Roderic Jeffries titles available from
Severn House Large Print

An Air of Murder
Definitely Deceased
An Intriguing Murder
Seeing is Deceiving

A SUNNY DISAPPEARANCE

A SUNNY DISAPPEARANCE

Roderic Jeffries

Severn House Large Print
London & New York

This first large print edition published in Great Britain 2006 by
SEVERN HOUSE LARGE PRINT BOOKS LTD of
9-15 High Street, Sutton, Surrey, SM1 1DF.
First world regular print edition published 2005 by
Severn House Publishers, London and New York.
This first large print edition published in the USA 2006 by
SEVERN HOUSE PUBLISHERS INC., of
595 Madison Avenue, New York, NY 10022.

British Library Cataloguing in Publication Data

Jeffries, Roderic, 1926-
    A sunny disappearance. - Large print ed. - (An Inspector
    Alvarez mystery)
    1. Alvarez, Enrique (Fictitious character) - Fiction
    2. Police - Spain - Fiction
    3. Detective and mystery stories
    4. Large type books
    I. Title
    823.9'14 [F]

ISBN-13: 9780727875501
ISBN-10: 0727875507

Printed and bound in Great Britain by
MPG Books Ltd, Bodmin, Cornwall.

One

Milne had just moved his chair, to escape the harsh sunshine which had begun to invade the small patio, when Sarah walked back out of the bungalow. 'Who phoned?' he asked.

She sat, picked up her glass, drank. 'Maurice,' she finally said.

'What did he want?'

'To invite us to a party.'

'You refused, of course?'

'No.' She drank quickly, emptied her glass. 'Why should I?'

'In the circumstances...'

'My God! Are we back to that again?'

His tone became pleading. 'Can't you understand how I feel?'

'It's impossible to know how you feel about anything.'

'But hearing about it for the first time from Leslie.'

She said scornfully: 'And you just listened instead of telling him what a creep he is, going around telling filthy rumours?'

He checked what he'd been about to say. If

5

he annoyed her too much, she would express her resentment later in bed. 'But why didn't you just mention it to me?'

'You're a needle stuck in the groove.'

'If you'd told me you'd been up at Maurice's place when Gloria was away and I was in the UK, I'd have laughed at Leslie. But learning about it from him and not you, makes it seem as if you've been trying to keep it secret from me.'

'It doesn't occur to you I forgot all about it because it was so unimportant and it was so unimportant because nothing happened?'

It had become too late to close the conversation. 'But with a man of Maurice's reputation...'

'His reputation! You're just one more sad old person with nothing better to do than swop envious rumours.'

'Each time Gloria goes off to Belgium—'

'Liechtenstein.'

'It doesn't make any difference where she goes.'

'It shows you don't know what the hell you're talking about.'

'Each time Gloria goes away, he has a woman up to his place.'

'That's a sick calumny.'

He did not miss the anger with which she had spoken.

'I suppose that's something more Leslie said and you rush to believe. You're pathetic!

I need another drink.' She picked up her glass.

She was a sun lover, ignoring health warnings, and wore a bikini top and a thong. As he watched her walk into the sitting room, her rounded flesh moving at each stride, he suffered an all too familiar rush of desire – a desire which often destroyed his self-respect. He went to drink, found his glass was empty; he considered following Sarah into the kitchen and refilling his glass, but lacked the gumption to face her. As he stared at the side wall of the next bungalow, seven metres away, he recalled how Jane, his first wife, had told him two days before she died, that she hoped he'd marry again because he needed someone to lean on. Doubtless, she had hazily envisaged a woman of around his age, probably a widow, who provided companionship and just sufficient sex to calm his desires. But he'd met Sarah, whose naturally wavy, blonde hair, shapely body, and suggestion of sexual adventures, had captivated him. He had lacked the sense to understand her character was immature and grasping and she judged him to be wealthy. Men who married women considerably younger than themselves wore fools' caps.

Tired of working all hours in order to keep his company viable in very difficult times, longing to pursue the dream of living in a sunny climate, he had suggested to Sarah that he sell his company and they move to Mallorca, where he and Jane had twice had memorable holidays. Sarah had been enthusiastic. He should have remembered that dreams survive only in dreams. The business had proved difficult to sell and the purchase price considerably less than he had hoped; the annuity had been more expensive than originally quoted because of the financial situation; only when looking for a house to buy, did he discover that the price of property in Mallorca had risen at an even greater rate than in England. Very soon after moving, he had belatedly realized Sarah's enthusiasm had been based on the mental picture of a luxurious house staffed by servants, a large garden and an exotically shaped swimming pool, not a bungalow with a tiny garden, no swimming pool, in an urbanización of dozens of broadly similar bungalows; she had imagined herself hosting exciting parties at which the rich and famous enjoyed champagne, caviare, foie gras, and smoked salmon, not dull parties at which ordinary people drank cava and ate the local pâté on Inca biscuits.

They had heard much about Maurice Rook – to his disadvantage – before they met him at a cocktail party given by an ex-army colonel, unusually with a pleasant wife. To their surprise – at least to his since he had never thought of himself as the kind of person people liked to meet – Maurice had invited them to one of his notable parties.

Son Raldo was a possessió, in Mayuorka Valley, to the north-west of Llueso. Once a thriving, self-sufficient estate, it had gradually declined as land was sold to meet gambling debts and the very large, stone-built house had fallen into disrepair. Rook had bought the house and the two dozen hectares of land which remained, had had the house renovated to the highest standards, and the land restored to fertility.

They'd joined the other guests around the large, kidney-shaped swimming pool, its mosaic tiling illuminated by underwater lights. Beyond the pool, a fountain jet, some five metres high – sheer luxury in a land of water shortage – provided the soothing sound of splashing water which had been so loved by the Moors. Staff, wearing white gloves, had poured champagne and offered titbits of foie gras, smoked salmon, and caviare, on silver salvers...

For days afterwards, Sarah's discontent had flowed. Their bedroom was far too small, the kitchen was poorly equipped, the only view out of the sitting room was of another miserable little box, the daily who came once a week for three hours wasn't worth half the eight euros an hour she now demanded, they drank cheap wine ... It had been several days before she had ceased to suffer from a headache in bed.

They'd met Rook again, some three weeks later, as they'd walked along the western arm of the harbour, now a marina. Rook had complimented her on her appearance, causing her to feign embarrassment to hide her satisfied pleasure. They'd been invited to have a drink aboard his boat.

When they'd finished the first bottle of Bollinger, he'd said he'd open another. Never overstay your welcome, had been one of Milne's mother's social guides, so he'd thanked Rook for the offer, but said they must leave and return home.

'Leave before the cellar's empty? That's not only careless, it's irresponsible.' Rook had turned to Sarah. 'You'd like some more bubbles to tickle the nose, wouldn't you?'

Her answer had been a giggle. One glass later, she'd begun to behave with alcoholic flirtatiousness. Milne had tried to make her realize she was acting stupidly, but if she'd received the message, she'd ignored it. When he'd refused the invitation to lunch at one of the local restaurants, she hadn't tried to hide her resentful annoyance. When they'd left the boat, she'd contemptuously refused his offer to help her down the gangplank, then would have fallen had he not supported her.

As they'd entered the tiny hall at home, she'd said: 'What a grotty little place this is!' Even then, he'd failed to realize the course her befuddled thoughts were taking...

Her return to the patio brought his mind back to the present. Glass in hand, she sat.

'I suppose you'll soon be demanding something to eat?'

He did not reply.

'A statue would make better company than you.' When she next spoke, her tone had become thoughtful rather than resentful. 'She was looking very sour yesterday, wasn't she?'

'Who are you meaning?'

'Gloria, of course. I wonder if there's trouble between her and Maurice? That wouldn't be surprising. She's hardly his type.'

'Anything female is his type.'

'You would say that. You're jealous of him. Which is why you go on and on suggesting ridiculous, beastly things.'

'Is it ridiculous to wonder why one's wife didn't mention she'd visited a man who was on his own?'

'I've told you a hundred times, he wasn't on his own. He never is. The place is swarming with servants.'

'Who will have learned from experience to keep out of sight and hearing.'

'You're sick! But if it'll ease your ridiculous jealousy, the butler chap served drinks and Gail was there.'

'You've never mentioned her before.'

'I didn't think I needed to. I stupidly

believed there was trust between us.'

'You're...' He stopped. He was convinced she was lying and Gail had not been at home.

'Well?' she demanded.

He didn't answer. He knew bitter, impotent anger, directed at her and Rook, but above all, at himself because he lacked the courage to accuse her of lying.

Two

Riera finally found a parking space on the eastern arm of the harbour. He switched off the engine of his Renault 5, stepped out on to the road and locked the car even though it was unlikely anyone would steal so ancient and distressed a vehicle.

He walked past the restaurant in which tourists were eating and reflected that many of them would be spending more on one meal than he earned in a week – a morose thought which was quickly banished by the slapping of halyards against masts, a sound to draw any seaman's mind back to the sea.

His father had been the most skilful fisherman working out of Port Llueso; he had known where each of the many species of fish was most likely to be found, what nets to use and when to cast. He'd spent days, even weeks, away from the family, living in a simple hut on the shore so that every hour could be used. His greatest skill had been exercised in catching the raor, that strange fish which dug itself into the sea bed. He'd pursued the llampugas when there was thunder and lightning because that was when they were most likely to be caught. On one such quest, the wind had suddenly become of storm intensity and he had drowned. Life for his mother, his three sisters, and him had become still harder, but because his father had begun to teach him how to fish, he had been able to relieve their poverty and, as time increased his skills, to provide even a little comfort...

If time had helped him in one respect, it had hurt in others. Improved means of refrigerated transport meant fish could be shipped in great quantities from Galicia and, coming from colder waters, there was far greater variety and better quality, so that, inevitably, locally caught fish had become less popular. The over-fishing necessary to combat the loss of earnings ensured ever diminishing catches. Laws, passed by men who did not risk their lives at sea, restricted the catching of crayfish and lobsters between September and March; the use of trawl nets was only permitted for six months...

Older fishermen, taking advantage of a state pension, had retired, middle-aged men had quit because there were far safer, easier, and better paid jobs to be found ashore in the tourist trade, young men had no thought of fishing. But he continued sailing in his llaüt, mostly on his own, occasionally with a hand, because in a muddled way he felt it necessary to continue the family tradition even though determined to be the last of the family to do so...

He had walked too far and he stopped. A man's memories could take him where he would rather not go. Abeam of him was a ten or twelve metre motor cruiser on which two men and two women were drinking. Sunday-sailors, he thought with brief contempt, aboard a boat with so much superstructure she would broach in a heavy wind and rough sea and go to the bottom. He turned and walked back to the boatyard, passed through the wide gateway. To his left were yachts in cradles, their hulls being scraped and painted and beyond them the hoist and shipway; to his right was a large shed, built four years before, on the side of which, in letters a metre high, was painted *Fiol y hijo*. He had been at school with Jorge Fiol. Being one of fourteen children, Fiol had been skinny from deprivation and had worn hand-me-down clothes. Now, he was one of the wealthiest of the local Mallorquins.

Inside the shed, several boats in cradles were being repaired and to the rough noise of machinery was added the roar of pop music. Used to the calm of the open sea, where the only sounds were the slap of water against the hull and the low whistle of wind in the rigging, Riera found the row physically unsettling. He searched for his llaüt and saw her at the far end of the shed, dwarfed by a large motor cruiser with bows and superstructure so raked, she gave the impression of speed even out of the water. No one was working on his boat. He walked forward, briefly returning the greeting of two men, and climbed the short flight of wooden stairs to the office. A young woman looked up from the computer at which she was working and told him Fiol was in the second, inner office. He went through to a room cooled by air-conditioning.

'Carlos! It's good to see you again.' Fiol leaned across his desk and held out his right hand.

Like shaking hands with a blancmange, Riera thought. The skinny boy in ragged clothes was now an overweight man dressed in expensive, contemporary-style clothes which would have suited someone half his size.

'Sit down and tell me how the world's treating you?'

'Not as well as it's obviously treating you,' Riera answered, as he settled on one of the two chairs in front of the desk.

'I've no complaints.' Fiol spoke with satisfaction. 'That is, when I'm not having to deal with Germans who have to be the most suspicious people on the earth. Present them with their account and they question even the commas.'

16

'Because you've made the bill read thous-
ands instead of the hundreds it should be?'

Fiol smiled and his cheeks creased into
folds of flesh.

'I came to see how my boat's coming
along. There's no one working on her, so
why the hell not?'

'Ah! There is a problem.'

'Of course there is. All the time she's not
afloat, I'm bloody well not earning.'

'We had a closer look at the damage and
it's greater than it appears. At least two of
the knee-timbers are going to have to be
replaced.'

Riera swore.

'It'll be quite a long job.'

'Made all the longer when you don't get
someone doing the work.'

'I'm afraid it's going to cost more than I
suggested.'

'How much more?'

'The best part of five thousand.'

'Are you crazy? I'm a fisherman, not some
foreign millionaire who's stupid enough to
pay ten times what the job's worth.'

'That's not a very friendly thing to say. It's
always been my policy to be completely
honest even when dealing with rich foreigners.'

Riera cursed his quick temper. 'I haven't
got five thousand euros.'

'Why should that matter? Señor Rook's

insurance company will pay up since you say his boat rammed yours.'

'The bastard's trying to say it was all my fault.'

'Of course he is.'

'But he was handling his boat like he was blind drunk.'

'Which, being English, he probably was.'

'He had a tart aboard who did all the talking because she spoke Spanish. She said I'd cut across his bows when he'd right of way. That's all balls.'

'His boat is much bigger than yours...'

'Like a bloody liner.'

'So maybe you should have let him have right of way. Still, you being a fisherman, likely the insurers will listen to you, not him.'

'She said his lawyers in Palma would fight any claim I tried to make. You think I can afford a lawyer to talk for me?'

'Maybe he had something like that in mind and was just talking to scare you off. But then, he's a rough hombre when it comes to money. Goes through a bill questioning everything. More like a German than an Englishman.'

'Whatever his nationality, he sailed straight into me.'

'He's really that incompetent at the helm?'

'Because he's stinking rich and means money to you, now you're saying it was my fault?'

'I'm not suggesting anything of the sort.'

'It sounded like you were. He was just going to carry on because he has a bloody big boat and I'm a poor fisherman in a thirty-five-year-old llaüt who'll get out of the way.'

'The rich think like that.'

'They don't give a damn about anyone else.'

'Why should they bother?'

'They reckon they can get away with anything.'

'With enough euros, that's the way life works.'

'I'll teach the bastard it doesn't.'

There was a silence, which Fiol broke. 'I'm over my head with work, so if that's all?'

'It's going to cost five thousand more?'

'Give or take a euro or two.'

'I ain't got that sort of money.'

'You mentioned. So forget going for his insurers and let your lot handle the matter.'

'I'm not covered for accidental damage.'

Fiol noisily drew in his breath. 'It's always dangerous not being fully insured.'

'I know that now, don't I?'

'Have a word with your bank; they'll likely help.'

'When fishing's become so bad, I hardly make enough to keep the family. Jorge, we've always been good friends since we were at school and—'

'Good friends since we were at school?'

19

Fiol spoke thoughtfully. 'Am I remembering wrongly when I think you were responsible for me being nicknamed "Scarecrow" because old clothing was mostly all I had to wear? And wasn't there a time when I was given a new shirt by an aunt and you and someone else – never can remember his name – rolled me around in the mud after some heavy rain because you said that otherwise you wouldn't be able to recognize me? Ah well, I'm sure it was only juvenile good fun. Now, were you going to ask me something?'

Riera had intended to ask for the work to be carried out at a favourable price and payment to be delayed, but it was obvious he might as well hope to dream the number of the winning lottery ticket. He was damned if he was going to give the other the further pleasure of refusing the request in soft words of regret, intended to wound still deeper. 'I can't remember what it was.'

'Then it can't have been important. There is just one thing. I've so much work in hand and on the books, I'll be grateful if you'll remove your boat if there's likely to be any delay ... You know, I often wonder why I work so hard. I mean, of what use is too much money at our age?'

Riera regretted he had done no more than furnish Fiol with a nickname and roll him in the mud.

Three

'I must check the meal,' Vivien said as she stood. 'I bought pork chops, hoping they won't be as tough as last time.' She turned and, followed by Isis – a Yorkshire terrier, walked from the balcony into the sitting room.

Isis was her shadow, Carr thought, as he picked up his glass and drank. Faced with the choice of losing him or Isis, it was possible she would hesitate for a second. He emptied his glass, replaced it on the patio table. Alcohol was said to provide false cheer. He would welcome a suggestion of cheer, however false. The sky might be cloudless, but his day was heavily overcast.

She returned, picked up Isis, sat. 'I said at the time, it was a crazy thing to do.' She fondled Isis's right ear.

'I know you did. But the way Maurice talked about the idea ... It seemed a chance not to be missed.'

'How he must have been laughing!'

He mentally winced. 'But...' He stopped.

'Well?'

'You're suggesting Maurice deliberately swindled me.'

'You think he didn't know there had to be a better reason than he gave you for the land to be offered so cheaply? He knew there was a chance it would be seized by someone else at less than was being asked because the autonomous government was going to pass a law giving some developers the right to buy at existing rather than potential value.'

'How could he know?'

'By using his common sense. He's very far from being a fool. He knew the land was being offered at far less than was being asked elsewhere. He reckoned it was a gamble and so he'd use other people's money to carry it out. If he bought and there was a requisition, they lost; if it wasn't requisitioned, he could carry out the development and cream off most of the profit.'

'You're accusing him of something almost criminal.'

'You think he became rich by behaving like a gentleman?'

'How does a gentleman behave these days?'

'He doesn't involve his friends in damming losses by playing on their greed.'

'It wasn't greed,' he protested.

'I know. I'm sorry, Derek, I shouldn't have said that. You panicked after sending all that money to Tom because he was in trouble through Vera's extravagance and then that damned insurance company went bust and your pension was threatened. But we could have managed. Yet now … Have you worked out how we stand financially?'

'Roughly.'

'And?'

'Things may become rather tight.'

'Stop havering and tell me the facts.'

'We're going to be on a rather reduced income.'

'When it's already difficult to manage with prices having gone through the roof since the change to the euro?'

'We may have to sell this place and buy a flat.'

'Move into a flat?' Her voice was high.

'So long as it's not overlooking the bay, it should leave us with a reasonable amount to put into something paying good interest.'

'Have you forgotten what Gwen said it was like when she moved into her flat? She hears almost every footstep because the people upstairs haven't any carpets on the floors, the noise from the bar on the other side of the road keeps her awake almost every night, the management charges keep going up when no work ever seems to be done, the drains are always stinking…'

'It was a very cheap flat.'

'Haven't you just said we're going to have to buy downmarket?'

'We should be able to find something nicer than she did.'

'I've never lived in a flat and I'm not going to do so now.'

'We may not have the choice.'

'A lot of flats won't allow dogs.'

'We'll find one that will.'

'And if we can't?' She stroked Isis with nervous energy.

'Sweet, let's not look on the black side of everything...'

'You want me to be very British and face disaster with a smiling upper lip?' She looked out at the roofs of the house below them, the part of Llueso which was visible, Puig Antonia on the top of which was the old hermitage, the distant jigsaw of small fields separated by dry-stone walls, the bay and its surrounding mountains. 'When we came here looking for a home, I was pursuing a dream.'

'I know.'

'You may know, but you understand nothing.' Isis looked up at her, surprised by the anger in her voice. She spoke more calmly. 'When we were shown this house, it was my dream in reality and I was frightened you wouldn't like it; when you said you did, I was ecstatic. I'd be able to sit on this balcony and look out at all the beauty so wonderfully different from suburban London, have a proper garden, swim in my pool...' She stopped.

'I'm so damned sorry.'

'It's not as if I didn't say time and again that it was ridiculous. But you wouldn't listen, wouldn't step back and understand he's too smooth, too hail-fellow-well-met, too self-satisfied, to be honest.'

'I knew he'd probably led a sharp life.'

'But that wasn't enough to warn you he's always ready to take advantage of anyone soft enough to trust him?'

'It wasn't as if he persuaded me to invest in the scheme.' Why was he trying to defend Rook? To lessen his own gullibility?

She put Isis on the floor, stood. 'I'm going to get the meal. I suppose you'll soon tell me we'll have to start living on chickpeas?'

He saw a tear slide down her cheek before she turned and left. He stared at the view without seeing it. That fatal luncheon. Champagne, a delicious meal accompanied by a really good Burgundy, followed by a 41-year-old Croft. After the second glass of port, Rook had mentioned he was considering buying fifty hectares of land in sight of, but a little back from, the sea, near Marbella. When surprise had been expressed, he'd explained the land was for sale at a very attractive price as the previous owner had died and left it to his son who was a gambler and needed money quickly. Rook had laughed. A good businessman would have asked slightly more than his land was worth to hide his need for ready cash. Harry had asked him what he intended to do with the land. Develop it, of course. And because that was going to cost serious money, he'd probably approach a few friends back in England to join in with him. He'd smiled. Those friends found very great difficulty in refusing to enjoy a threefold or fourfold profit...

Carr had told Vivien that here was their chance to repair their finances. She had spoken against the idea, being unable to appreciate the sense of humiliation he suffered because their standard of living had dropped. He'd asked Rook if he could join the scheme. After evident – it had appeared evident – hesitation, Rook had finally agreed. Carr had withdrawn all their capital that was in a high-interest account in Jersey, convincing himself that soon they would no longer have to judge whether they could buy what they wanted and he could once more offer Vivien the small luxuries she so enjoyed...

Rook, 'honouring the partnership', had shown him the escritura for the land. A firm of architects had been commissioned to draw up the development plans. And then, using the new law imposed by the autonomous government – a law branded illegal by Spaniards as well as foreigners – the fifty acres had been compulsorily bought from them by a Spanish developer who had paid compensation for scrubland, a sum very much smaller than Rook had paid the feckless son.

Susan called out: 'Lunch.'

He stood, went into the sitting room and over to the small open-plan dining area. There was cold York ham, serrano ham, boiled potatoes, and beans on the table. He helped himself, poured out a glass of Bach, returned to the balcony.

When she joined him, he noticed how little food was on her plate. 'Aren't you hungry?'

'No.'

He wanted to say something to cheer her up, could think of nothing. They'd not enjoyed a very prosperous life after their marriage and had lived in a small terraced house for some years before they'd been able to move to a semi-detached in Southgate. Then an aunt had died and left him an unexpected legacy and he had taken early retirement. They had come out to the island and bought the house which previously could only be hers in her dreams. Now they were going to have to sell and move on. He wasn't as convinced as she that Rook had swindled him, but that didn't lessen his hatred for the other.

Four

They sat in the shade of the pool complex.

'I wish to God we didn't have to,' Gloria said.

They wouldn't, Rook thought, if he'd remembered what he knew – all authority was crooked.

'Are you really sure we've got to do this?'

'Unless you want to live like one of the pension proles.'

'But I'm so worried.'

'There's no call to be.' She'd play her part well. He was banking his future that she would. Her looks and behaviour might brand her more beautiful than brainy, but in truth she was determined and intelligent. Very determined. After some bastard had hinted to her that on one of her visits to Liechtenstein he had not been lonely in bed, she had given him verbal hell, imitating an enraged fishwife. That had annoyed him. It was a woman's duty to keep a man happy and to understand he needed fresh tastes to awaken a jaded palate. When she'd told him what she thought of that sexist crap, he'd considered getting rid of her. But to his annoyance, he'd discovered how reluctant he was to do that. So he'd restored relations by giving her the jade brooch she had seen and so admired in a Palma jeweller's...

She picked the bottle of Veuve Clicquot out of the cooler and refilled their glasses. 'Why are you looking at me like that?' she asked, as she replaced the bottle.

'I was wondering whether to have a quick one before lunch.'

'A swim?'

'Be your age.'

She giggled. 'I'm going in the pool, so come in with me.'

'Too dangerous.'

'Why?'

'Gaspar might arrive at the moment critique.'

'It's not like you to be embarrassed.'

'Embarrassment isn't the point.'

'Then what is?'

'I employ him, so I'm not providing him with some free voyeuristic enjoyment.'

'You can be a hard man, Maurice,' she said, not as lightly as intended.

'It's not a world for the soft.'

She drank, replaced the glass on the table, stood and went out of the shade into the harsh sunshine.

He watched her walk around the pool to the diving board. Blonde hair, blue eyes, a

29

mouth made for many enjoyments, a swan's neck, pert breasts, a figure to excite a misogynist ... He'd known other women as arrogantly attractive – money ensured that – but she was the first to make him value her. This annoyed him.

She swam several lengths with a stylish crawl which suggested expert training. Yet, if she told the truth, until she'd met him, she'd had little chance to enjoy swimming. She reached the shallow end and climbed the steps, reminding him of the Birth of Venus. If all goddesses were born like her, he'd put his name down to be a god.

As she crossed the pool patio, the heat and dryness of air were such that she was hardly damp as she sat. She went to refill her glass, found the bottle was almost empty. She stood, walked into the main area of the complex and across to the refrigerator behind the small bar. 'There isn't another bottle down here,' she called out.

'Phone up and tell them to bring one down.'

She did so, returned to her chair. 'Sweetie, I really am worried.'

'So you've said, repeatedly.'

'But if the police become suspicious...'

'When they're so thick they don't know whether today is yesterday or tomorrow?'

'Something could so easily go wrong.'

'Not when I'm running things.'

'I wish it hadn't happened.'

'You think I'm all smiles?'

'I so love living here.'

'You'll enjoy the Bahamas more.'

'I don't know.'

'Then you're going to find out unless you'd rather we stay on here with no more money than most of them have?' Would she then find another patron? How much of her loyalty was he buying, how much was she offering for free?

'You're certain nothing can go wrong?'

'You want me to make a statement in front of a notario?' His brief anger was due to his own uneasiness. The best laid plans not only could go astray, the sharp mind accepted they all too frequently did. Yet he had planned, checked, double-checked...

Gail came into view as she rounded a centuries-old olive tree, transplanted to its present position at great cost. She had a brisk athletic stride, which reminded him of one of the women who had taught him at school – when he'd bothered to attend. Another similarity was that they both displayed the same quiet, good humour in the face of provocation and seldom, if ever, revealed their thoughts. Did Gail ever wonder if he had swindled her father, his brother, despite his assurances it had been business circumstances beyond anyone's control which had led to the loss? Did she resent his wealth?

31

Did she scorn his lifestyle, condemn his licentiousness? It was impossible to judge.

She came to a halt, lifted out the empty bottle from the cooler, replaced it with the unopened one she had brought. 'I've carried it as carefully as a baby, but you'd better still be ready for it to gush.'

'There wasn't another bottle in the frig,' Gloria said sharply.

'So I gathered when you asked me to bring this down.' She smiled.

The only time he would have judged her attractive was when she smiled. Even then, when in Gloria's company she remained the typical housewife.

'I've said I always want a couple of bottles in the frig down here,' Gloria said.

'And there were until you had friends to drinks last night.'

'They should have been replaced this morning.'

'And would have been, had I remembered.'

He was not surprised that she met ill-tempered criticism with good humour. Just like Helen, her mother. He'd always disliked Helen because she had never hidden her opinion of him.

'We'll have lunch at two,' Gloria said.

'I think Luisa was working to one thirty. I'll tell her to slow things down.'

She still showed no resentment at Gloria's curt manner. Deliberately depriving Gloria of the satisfaction of upsetting her?

Gail turned to leave.

'Did you tell the butcher the last joint of beef was too tough to eat?' Gloria demanded.

'Yes.'

'Well, what did the man say?'

'We English are always complaining about something because we are so sour.'

'What absolute insolence! What did you do?'

'I laughed.'

'Hardly an expression of propriety.'

'In high society?'

'What do you mean?'

'Isn't there a song about propriety in high society?'

'I've no idea ... Tell Marta our bedroom wasn't cleaned properly yesterday. There was dust on the back of the dressing-table. She's becoming lazier and lazier.'

'She's distracted because of trouble at home.'

'That's hardly our concern. She's paid to do a job and if she doesn't do it, she'll have to go.'

'I wouldn't suggest that. She's normally reliable and is completely honest. It's become difficult to find such staff. Her home life will probably sort itself out.'

'You're always finding excuses for the staff.'

'Blame a sympathetic understanding of their problems.'

'Is that supposed to mean something?'

'Not really.' Gail left.

Gloria watched her as she walked up the gently sloping lawn, past the olive tree. 'She can be bloody annoying.'

'One of the few feminine virtues she enjoys.'

'She was trying to be insolent when she said she had a sympathetic understanding of the servants' problems.'

'Possibly.' He stood, lifted the bottle out of the cooler, stripped off the foil and wire cage, eased out the cork, refilled their glasses. 'Whatever happens, make certain you follow the timetable.' He sat. 'Phone Charles and Hilda...'

'For God's sake, not again.'

'Again.'

'But—'

'You phone and ask to speak to me. You're told I haven't arrived. You ring again and express growing worry, you've tried to get me on the boat's radio phone and there's no answer. If you speak to Charles, he'll talk about adverse currents, blocked fuel lines, radio gremlins, and navigational incompetence. You'll ring a third time and become slightly hysterical because you're sure something's wrong and what on earth can you do?'

'I hope...' She stopped.

'Hope on, hope ever.'

She drained her glass. 'I'm going to have another swim. You're not coming in?'

'As I said.'

He watched her cross the patio and dive in. There were few pleasures to equal that of observing a beautiful woman and know one would soon be quenching one's desires with her; the wait added to the pleasure. His mind swung to the future. Of course, the insurance company would make enquiries and the police would investigate, but even were they competent, he was certain they would learn nothing but the obvious.

He refilled his glass. It was ironic that the present trouble had arisen when, for once, he had been operating with complete honesty. His scheme to buy the land and develop it had been backed by professional advice. He had invested most of his capital and only accepted money from others with reluctance and the amused condescension that he would let them enjoy a little financial sunshine. He should have remembered that to reach too far was to overbalance. But how was he to know the autonomous government would allow the land to be legally stolen from him by some bastard who wanted to develop it himself?

Gloria climbed out of the pool and crossed to her chair. 'The water's over thirty ... Will it be as hot in the Bahamas?'

'Hotter maybe.'

'They have hurricanes, which will be terribly scary.'

'I'll hold you tight. Whatever happens, don't try to get in touch...'

'I'm not stupid, Maurice.'

'Even if the heavens threaten to fall, don't phone, fax, email, or write, however safe you think yourself. Just stay silent, shed tears, have a nice memorial service for me, and tell everyone you can't bear to stay here with all the memories and put the house up for sale through agents, even if they're bloody robbers when it comes to their commission. As soon as it's sold, get the money transferred to our account in Liechtenstein and set sail.'

'What about the staff here?'

'You'll probably have to pay them redundancy money – add something so they remember us with gratitude. And give Gail a couple of thousand and a kiss on each cheek.'

'Why give her anything? You've done enough for her.'

'If she's thrown out cold, people might start thinking and wondering and we want everyone to remain in their normal state of mental stupor ... Having done all that, you rent somewhere in England and live there for a few months before you tell the inquisitive neighbours you're off to sit at the feet of a guru to learn how to come to terms with your fractured soul.'

'Say that and people will think I'm daft.'

'Or freaked out on pot. In either case, no one will give a damn what happened to you and that you did not fly out to Kathmandu.'

'Why would I go to Burma?'

He smiled.

'Why are you laughing at me?'

'Admiration.'

'Sometimes I just can't understand you.'

'The recipe for a perfect relationship.'

'Maurice...'

'Well?'

'If you start up with another woman before I get to the Bahamas, I'll kill the bitch.'

'But after your arrival, she'll be quite safe? I foresee a perfect ménage à trois.'

Five

Alvarez stared at the mail on his desk and noticed one letter still had not been opened – it was unlikely to be important. He yawned and his eyelids became heavy, but if he fell asleep, he might not awaken until well after it was time to leave.

The phone rang. Phones were the invention of the devil, invading a man's privacy. Since it kept ringing, he finally lifted the receiver. 'Yes?'

'Is that you, Enrique?'

Instinct told him the call was going to cause work. 'Who's speaking?' he demanded bad-temperedly.

'Andrés, down in the port.'

It took him several seconds to identify López, a member of the Policia Local, an earnest man who lacked the ability to take life at a rewarding pace. 'How's the family?'

'Eulalia's been having trouble.'

'Serious?'

'Women's trouble, so I wouldn't know; makes her mighty sharp, though.'

She was too sharp even when untroubled,

Alvarez reflected.

'But Tolo and Rosa are fine and at school she's top of her form and he's not far short of the same. Makes a man proud. There's nothing like having children.'

'So they tell me.' They also told him that children made a wife so tired she went to bed to sleep; they cost so much, the husband had also to forgo many of the other pleasures he had been enjoying.

'D'you know what Tolo said the other day? This will make you laugh...'

He dutifully laughed.

'But to work. We've just had a foreign woman – English – come in and say her husband's gone missing in his boat and wants us to find him. Sailed from the port at eleven and, according to her, should have reached Mahon before eighteen hundred hours when he would have phoned her. He didn't, so she got in touch with the people he was going to visit and they said there was no sign of him. She's tried and failed to rouse him on the radio.'

Alvarez looked at his watch. 'Not all that long overdue. Probably stopped out at sea for a swim.'

'I did suggest that, but she says he's on his own.'

'What difference does that make?'

'There speaks a real landlubber! You never leave a boat at sea when there's no one else

39

aboard. If there's a wind or a current, the boat can drift away from you faster than you can swim towards it.'

Alvarez pictured himself in the middle of the sea, his boat inexorably drifting away from him so that death sat on his shoulders. He mentally shivered.

'As I said, she's demanding we organize a search, but I can't see it's our problem.'

'Likewise, it's not ours.'

'Then what do I do?'

'Inform the harbourmaster.'

'Shouldn't we do something more?'

'You'll have to be the judge of that.' Alvarez skilfully brought the conversation to an end, replaced the receiver. His imagination raced. Panic overwhelmed him as the boat drifted further out of reach, his strength ebbed, and it slowly became too much of an effort to keep his face above the water ... For once he was glad to return to the office.

He made his way out of the post and along to his car. As he drove, he mused on the strange fact that time and distance were elastic – the trip home was always shorter than the trip to work.

In the dining/sitting room, Jaime, his expression disgruntled, sat at an empty table. Alvarez settled opposite him. 'Have you decided to go on the water wagon?' he asked facetiously.

Dolores called out from the kitchen: 'You

can believe the impossible?' She stepped through the bead curtain. Her midnight-black hair was in some disarray, there was a smudge of flour on her cheek and she wore a patched apron over her dress, but her air of justified superiority would have equalled that of any exotically fashioned Andaluce beauty at the feria. 'As I have told my husband, supper will be late. You will not, naturally, be in the slightest interested why. What man concerns himself with the problems a woman meets?'

If he did, Alvarez thought, he'd have no time to live. He wondered if a few thoughtful words might blunt her aggression? 'I hope the trouble wasn't anything serious?'

'No doubt your hope arises from the fear that if it was, I might be unable to serve anything other than garbanzos. As my mother used to say, a woman can as soon look for selfless sympathy from a man as honesty from a politician. Of course, in her day, all politicians were men.' She returned into the kitchen.

In her present mood, Alvarez thought with sudden gloom, it was just possible that she would serve chickpeas, which, no matter how tasty the sauce, remained chickpeas. He leaned forward to speak in an undertone. 'What's got her going this time?'

'How the hell would I know?' Jaime answered.

Didn't it occur to him, Alvarez wondered, that as her husband, it was his duty to correct her attitude?

'All she said was supper would be late and that wasn't an excuse for drinking.'

'That doesn't prevent you enjoying a small drink now.'

'I suppose not.'

Why couldn't Jaime be more of a man? Alvarez leaned over and opened a sideboard door, brought out a bottle of Soberano which he put down on the table carefully so that it did not make a noise and alert Dolores; he lifted out one glass at a time for fear that two together might clink. He poured out two generous brandies. He would have liked to add several ice cubes to his drink, but that would have meant going into the kitchen.

The phone rang.

'One of you can answer,' Dolores called out. It was a command, not a suggestion.

'It won't be for me,' Jaime said.

And, Alvarez thought as he stood, he hoped it wasn't for him.

Hopes were like sandcastles, easily washed away. 'It's Andrés. I've had the English señora here again. Her husband still hasn't arrived at Mahon.'

Alvarez looked at his watch. 'Then maybe he's not going to ... You informed the harbourmaster?'

'Tried to make out it wasn't his responsibility.'

'Lazy bastard!'

'But I think he's organized some sort of a search.'

'Then there's nothing more can be done.'

'What about the wife? Shouldn't someone tell her there's a search in progress?'

'Who is she?'

'Señora Rook. I told you that.'

'I mean, what kind of person?'

'Can't really answer. It seems his boat's one of the biggest in the port, so there's plenty of money.' López's tone became resentful. 'Why do foreigners cause trouble all the time?'

'Because that's all they're any good at.'

'Life was much easier in the old days when there weren't any of them.'

'But much harder without their money.'

'Things are never smooth, are they?'

'Not for ordinary people like us,' Alvarez agreed sadly.

A moment later, he returned to the dining room. The meal was on the table. Cordero estofado and not a garbanzo in sight.

43

Six

On Thursday morning, López replaced the receiver and stared blankly at the wall of his room in the Policia Local building. The boat had been found five nautical miles off Cap Parelona and since there was no sign of its owner, it had to be presumed he had drowned while trying to free the starboard propeller which had become entangled with a length of fisherman's net.

He drummed on the desk with his fingers. He knew what it was now his duty to do, but had seldom been so reluctant to do it. He was too soft-hearted to be a policeman, even if the work of the Policia Local was normally restricted to regulating local traffic, controlling markets, enforcing rules regarding hygiene, and ceremonial duties. He was being called upon to be a harbinger of tragedy. He stopped drumming and stood. A man had to do what a man had to do. And he had to drive to Son Raldo.

A modest person, with much to be modest about, he and Margarita lived in the village house given to her by her parents which he had spent four years restoring before her parents said they might marry. Now that they had four children and a fifth was due, their home had become very small. Son Raldo seemed to him to be little short of a palace and once inside, the luxury of the furnishings increased his nervousness.

Gloria entered the morning room, its marble floor partially in sunlight. Deeming it advisable to dress with restraint, she wore one of her more modest costumes. López was undecided whether she looked like a model or a whore.

'You've some news?' she asked in reasonable Spanish.

'Yes, señora.' Since she was English, he presumed she was not married, but at such a time it was only proper to offer her the courtesy of marriage. 'It has just been given to me.'

'My husband's safe?'

No one had taught him how to deliver bad news compassionately. 'We don't know.'

'Why not?'

'Señora, the boat has been found at sea, off Cap Parelona, and no one was aboard.'

'You're not saying ... That's impossible ... Something went wrong, so he tried to use the ship-to-shore radio, but it wouldn't work – it's always going wrong – so he went ashore in the tender to call for help. The tender wasn't in the stern davits, was it?'

45

She'd used some English words and he'd no idea what she meant.

'Was the inflatable at the stern?'

'I ... I cannot say.'

'Why not? For God's sake...' She became silent. When she spoke again, it was in a low voice. 'He would have phoned me from ashore.' She crossed to one of the four stylishly modern chairs and slumped down on it. 'He was sailing to Mahon.'

'So I understand, señora.'

'He should have arrived hours ago. If he'd gone ashore after breaking down, he would ... he would...' She turned her head away from him.

He could not see if tears were sliding down her cheeks, but had no doubt they were. He wished himself anywhere but where he was, forced to share a woman's grief.

Eventually, he said apologetically: 'I must leave, señora.'

She did not respond.

'I will work day and night until...' Until the body was found?

He could not escape the house of sorrow quickly enough.

The heat and humidity sapped a man's strength and left him unable to work. Alvarez adjusted the fan to try to gain a fraction more benefit from its draught, settled back in the chair, put his feet up on the desk, closed

46

his eyes. He was about to drift into sleep when the phone jerked him fully awake.

He lifted the receiver. 'Yes?'

'Andrés here. I thought you'd want to know she's been found.'

'Who?'

'*Corrina.*'

'Didn't know she was missing.'

'I told you.'

'You most certainly have not told me some girl had gone missing.'

'*Corrina* is the boat belonging to Señor Rook.'

'Then why confuse me by saying "she" had been found?'

'The English call boats "she".'

'Typical! Tells you all you don't want to know about them. The boat's found, so what about the señor?'

'He's still missing. The starboard propeller had become entangled in a piece of netting, so it's likely he went overboard to try to free it and couldn't get back.'

'No body has turned up?'

'Not yet.'

'Have you spoken to the señora?'

'Yes, and it's something I never want to have to do again because...'

'I know. Not a pleasant task. Then that's the end of things as far as we're concerned.' He said goodbye, replaced the receiver, returned his feet to the desk, closed his eyes.

Seven

Experts agreed temperatures could rise no further, so they rose even though it was still not July. Trees as well as crops and animals were beginning to suffer except where there was abundant irrigation and only the tourists on the beaches enjoyed the piercing sunshine and they, unless reasonably intelligent, soon learned there was a price to pay if one sunbathed for long in the clear air – a price chemists and doctors were happy to receive.

Four days to the start of his holiday. Alvarez used a handkerchief to wipe the sweat from his face and neck and wondered if one could buy a ticket to the Arctic. Bliss would it be that dawn to be cool! The phone rang. An even greater bliss, to live in a world where the telephone had not been invented.

The superior chief's secretary spoke as if through a mouthful of plums; her manner expressed disdain for mere inspectors. 'Superior Chief Salas will speak to you.'

He waited.

Salas said angrily: 'Are you there?'

'Yes, señor.'

'Then why the devil don't you say so?'

'I was waiting...'

'To wait is to fail to arrive. Had you ever been able to understand that, your career in the Cuerpo might possibly have shown some promise ... I have received a request from England for our co-operation and have agreed to this, despite my natural disinclination to work with people for whom hypocrisy is a way of life. You will meet Señor Noyes and give him all assistance, making certain he does not involve the Cuerpo in any disreputable publicity, waste of time, or unnecessary expense.'

'Assist him in what, señor?'

'Must I constantly have to repeat myself? Señor Noyes works in a security organization which operates in the insurance field.'

There was a silence.

'Well?'

'Señor, I still don't understand.'

'Señor Rook had insured his life for a million pounds and his wife, who is his beneficiary, has informed the insurance company of his disappearance in circumstances which suggest death. However, the lack of a body, together with the sum insured, immediately raises the possibility of fraud. Your task is to help Señor Noyes determine whether that possibility can be ignored or is to be pursued. Have I explained in sufficiently simple terms for you to understand?'

'Yes, señor.'

Salas cut the connection.

Alvarez replaced the receiver, settled back in the chair. A million pounds. Whilst decades of inflation meant such a sum was no longer wealth beyond measure, it remained sufficient to enable a man to retire, buy a finca with many hectares of land, grow almonds, olives, lemons, oranges, pomegranates, figs, peppers, lettuces, cabbages, cauliflowers, tomatoes, beans, peas ... The dream vanished. This million pounds called for one's death.

He again used his handkerchief to wipe away the sweat. As he lowered it, he remembered something. He lifted the receiver, dialled.

'Superior Chief Salas's office,' the secretary said, in tones of a royal announcement.

'It's Inspector Alvarez. I must speak to the superior chief.'

'Wait.'

He waited.

'Yes?' said Salas.

'Señor, you know you told me I was to assist Señor Noyes?'

'Unlike some, I am always well aware of what I've said.'

'When does he arrive?'

'Monday.'

'Then I can't meet or work with him.'

'What the devil are you talking about?'

'I start my holiday on Monday.'

There was a long silence before Salas said: 'Due to circumstances, it is impossible to replace you, despite the benefit to the investigation that would ensue, so you will defer your holiday. I am sorry.' The line went dead.

Alvarez stared through the open and unshuttered window at the blank wall of the building on the other side of the street. Salas's words of regret had been laced with hypocrisy. Perhaps there was English blood in his veins.

'Enrique, you've hardly spoken,' Dolores said, as the family sat around the dining-room table. There was a note of worry in her voice. Let any of them suffer as little as a muscle twinge and she would envisage a medical emergency.

'Uncle's thinking of women,' Juan said pertly.

'Be quiet.'

'He—'

'Another word and you go straight up to bed.'

Isabel smiled mockingly. Juan tried to kick her ankle.

Dolores studied Alvarez more closely. 'Are you feeling all right?'

'As well as can be expected,' he replied glumly.

'Afraid she's met someone half your age and twice as good looking?' Jaime sniggered.

Dolores stood. 'Sweet Mary, but my mother was right when she said a woman would die an old maid if she waited to marry a man who would warm her life.'

'Can't I make a joke?' Jaime asked.

She ignored him. 'Juan, you can clear the plates.'

'But it's Isabel's turn to do that.'

'I see you have already learned from your father's example that it is never a man's job to do anything.'

'That's unfair!' Jaime said.

She again ignored him, picked up the serving dish and went through to the kitchen.

Jaime refilled his glass with wine. 'Doesn't matter what you say or do...'

Dolores returned, an earthenware bowl filled with oranges and apples in her hands. She put this down on the table, straightened up, spoke to Alvarez. 'Why do you say you are only as well as can be expected?'

'I've had some terrible news.'

'She's discovered she's...' Jaime stopped in mid-sentence, having noted Dolores's expression.

She sat, helped herself to an orange and began to peel it. 'What is the terrible news?'

'Salas has said I'm to meet an Englishman when he flies in on Monday and I'm to work with him.'

'But that's when it's your holiday. Surely you reminded the superior chief of the fact?'

'Of course I did.'

'Then what did he say?'

'That I was no longer starting it on Monday.'

'He's no right to do such a thing.'

'He disagrees.'

She divided up the orange and ate a segment. 'It did not occur to you that since he is always complaining about money spent unnecessarily, it would have been a good idea to suggest you had booked a holiday abroad and if you could no longer go on it, the Cuerpo would have to repay you what it had cost?'

Jaime said, 'And you call men deceivers!'

'Are you incapable of understanding men deceive for their own pleasures, women to help others?'

'You could fool me.'

'With no difficulty ... Enrique, you must inform the superior chief you may well suffer a nervous breakdown if you don't have a holiday after working so hard.'

'I doubt he'd believe that.'

'Expect the worst and the worst will happen.'

'It usually happens whether or not it's expected.'

★ ★ ★

53

Perello was a short, plump, hairy man who suffered from halitosis; his nickname was Pero, a laboured pun on 'perro'. He resembled an overfed Pekinese.

'Not had the pleasure for quite a time,' he said, as he shook hands.

'Nor have I,' replied Alvarez, who was standing within reach of the other's breath.

'So is it the Englishman's disappearance which brings you here?'

'It is.' Alvarez stepped back.

'Then have a seat. It's not the weather to stand about.'

Alvarez sat, briefly looked out of the window which provided a panoramic view of the harbour.

'What do you want to know?' Perello asked.

'The condition of the boat.'

'The finder's yacht hadn't the power to tow, so he just reported the *Corrina* adrift. March went out and before bringing it in, had a quick check. Everything was in order except that the starboard propeller had fishing net wound around it.'

'How would that have become caught up?'

'Who can answer? Nets get torn and bits fall to the bottom or drift around – there's no saying.'

'There's nothing unusual in a propeller being caught up in net?'

'I've known it to happen two or three times

54

over the past couple of years. A Frenchman blamed me when he picked up some halfway to Ibiza.'

'What kind of boat is it?'

'A thirty-metre Benetti with twin diesels and generous accommodation in luxury style – a beautiful job. Have you any idea how much fuel it consumes?'

'No.'

'At twelve to thirteen knots, it'll be around a hundred and fifty litres an hour.'

'Good grief!'

'Aye, you need money even to imagine owning something like it.'

Alvarez briefly considered a life in which one was so rich one could enjoy absurdly expensive luxuries. 'If it has two engines, there are two propellers?'

'It would be a funny layout if it didn't.'

'Couldn't the Englishman have used one engine to return?'

'The boat would try to sheer all the time, so steering would be difficult, but probably far from impossible.'

'Then why didn't he return on one engine, instead of going into the water to clear the propeller?'

'Boat owners, especially foreigners, are half crazy – have to be to waste their money like they do. Maybe he didn't want to limp back to port leaving a wake like a rollercoaster. They worry far more about their image than any car owner does.'

'What was the sea like?'

'Wet and salty.' Perello laughed loudly.

Alvarez received a further, if fainter, flavour of the other's breath.

'Was it calm?'

'Yes.'

'Can you be certain?'

'Of course I can, but I suppose you want me to check?'

'If you would.'

'You lot have to climb up and down a mountain before you'll admit it's there.' He stood and walked over to a cupboard, brought out a large, leather-bound log book. 'What was the date?'

Alvarez tried to remember.

'June the sixteenth, wasn't it?'

If it wasn't, that wouldn't be very far out.

'Swell slight, sea calm, wind force one, visibility excellent, sky cloudless, air temperature twenty-six and sea temperature twenty-one.'

'What does slight swell mean?'

'A bit of movement, but not much.'

'So the boat would roll a little?'

'Not enough to make you wonder if you should have eaten so much breakfast.'

'It wouldn't cause a man to lose his balance?'

'A landlubber like him can fall arse over tip in a flat calm. He knew as much about the sea as I do about satellites. Look at the way he ran into Riera's old llaüt. Maybe he did have right of way – not being there, I don't know – but a seaman would have kept clear when running down on a boat with the handling of a hippopotamus.'

'You're saying it's perfectly feasible Señor Rook lost his balance because of the boat's movements and he fell overboard?'

'Enrique, if someone told me he'd forgotten which way the boat's bows would turn if he put on port helm, I'd believe it.'

Life had taught Alvarez that while pleasure was sharply rationed, pain was in unlimited supply, yet even so, he had been shocked to learn Noyes's plane arrived at eight in the morning, which necessitated his leaving Llueso by seven. The coffee and brandy he bought at the airport might have restored a degree of inner harmony had he not been charged three times as much as he would have been in Llueso.

He left the bar and checked one of the overhead screens – a thirty-five minutes delay for the plane from Gatwick. About to return to the bar, he remembered Traffic had begun a campaign, carried out on the autoroutes and main roads, against driving when over the limit – a limit thought up by a comedian – and there was random breath-alysing. Even though it was so early in the

57

day, there would be those in Traffic who were cursed with enthusiasm. He bought a copy of *El Dia* and read, gained perverse pleasure from evidence there were those whose lives were even more blighted than his.

The thirty-five minutes delay became fifty minutes, then sixty-five. The plane was finally listed as having landed and passengers would be leaving by Gate 31. He had to walk a couple of hundred metres. After a few minutes, the overhead screen recorded a change to Gate 12. A long walk back. Then it became Gate 25. Even by the airport's own standards, such uncertainty was unusual. He swore, wearily trudged to Gate 25. It proved to be the last change of venue and passengers were beginning to come through into the arrival hall and congregate around the carousel.

He spoke to the guard at the doors and said he'd go through to meet a passenger. The guard did not hide his satisfaction when he said his orders were that no one, not even a member of the Cuerpo, was allowed to pass through.

Alvarez sat on one of the uncomfortable seats. A day which had begun ill could only become worse. Noyes would prove to be one of those tall, thin Englishmen with a toothbrush moustache, a manner expressing contempt for all garlic-eating foreigners, a vegan, a committed teetotaller...

Noyes was no taller than Alvarez, his waist-line as generous; he was clean shaven, his manner warm and friendly, and one of his first remarks was to express his anticipation of enjoying the local food and wine.

For lunch, Alvarez chose a restaurant in the old part of Llueso. It had never gained a Michelin star, but the chef's sopes, lomo con col, rijones al sal, or lechona asada, deserved four. In addition, the mark-up on wine was so low as to be justifiable.

'Another coñac?' Alvarez asked, as the one-eyed waiter cleared the last of the dishes.

'After all I've drunk?' Noyes answered.

'It will aid the digestion.'

'You've persuaded me.'

Alvarez ordered two more brandies.

'I can't remember when I've enjoyed a meal more,' Noyes said. 'And made all the more memorable because ... Tell the truth and shame the devil. I was afraid I'd be meeting someone who didn't speak English and who obviously resented having to work with me. It's funny how one has false impressions.'

'Very strange,' Alvarez agreed.

The waiter put two glasses down on the table, left. About to offer a cigarette, Alvarez remembered Noyes did not smoke; he lit one. 'I will try to get to your hotel by five.'

'You're tied up for the afternoon?'

He considered the question. 'You do not enjoy a siesta?'

'Normally, no. But I've always followed the wise advice that when in Rome do as the Romans do, most especially if one has dined and wined extravagantly.'

Playa de Llueso, built some forty years ago, enlarged and refurbished ten years ago, fronted the bay. Alvarez took the lift up to the fifth and top floor, walked along the passage to room 34, knocked on the door, entered.

Noyes, who had been sitting on one of the two cane chairs on the balcony, met him in the middle of the twin-bedded room.

'Did you have a good siesta?' Alvarez asked.

'A sybaritic one, thanks to the certainty that if I were at home, there are a dozen and one things which I would have to do.' He gestured at the French windows. 'This is Arcadia!'

Alvarez stared across the road at the beach, the poster-blue waters of the bay, and the surrounding mountains which provided so dramatic a background. 'I sometimes wonder if heaven is as beautiful as this.'

'If so, lead me there, but not just yet. I'd like to pay off the mortgage first.' Noyes smiled and his plump face wrinkled, adding to his air of good humour. It needed an alert observer to appreciate that behind the geniality was a sharp mind. 'So what do we do now?'

'I thought perhaps you would like to go for a drive and see a little of the island?'

'You don't think we ought to ... No, of course you don't. I'm forgetting, this is the Island of Calm.'

Next morning, Alvarez parked in front of the hotel on a solid yellow line. The receptionist said Noyes was in the lounge.

'Shall we have a coffee?' Alvarez suggested, after shaking hands. 'And it is the custom to have a small coñac with it.'

'There are some customs I rush to follow. But there's a proviso. This time, it's on me.'

Remembering Salas's comments on expenses, Alvarez did not argue.

A waiter took their order.

'I wonder if this would be a good moment to swop what information we have?'

Alvarez sighed. The English were always in a rush. 'I fear I have little to offer. I never had reason to meet Señor Rook or his wife and the most I can do is to confirm that he left here in his boat at about eleven on Wednesday morning to sail to Mahon. That evening, Señora Rook reported to the police he had not arrived and asked for a search to be made. *Corrina* – his boat – was found by a

61

fisherman roughly five nautical miles off Cap Parelona on Thursday and there was no one aboard it ... That is wrong.'

'There was someone aboard?'

'I called the boat "it", but I am told the English think all boats are feminine. Is that so?'

'It is.'

'Do you know why this should be when a boat surely needs to be strong and predictable?'

'Now I come to think about it, I've no idea.'

'Every nationality has its peculiarities,' Alvarez said generously.

'You say you haven't spoken to Mrs Rook?'

'The sad news of finding *Corrina* unmanned – if indeed it was sad news – was given to her by a member of the Policia Local. We can talk to him and ask him for his impressions of that meeting.'

The waiter returned with coffees and brandies, set them on the table.

'I should like to know how she received the news.' Noyes added sugar and milk to the coffee, drank, held the glass of brandy in his hand to warm it. 'Shall I tell you how things are at our end?'

'I should be grateful.'

'As you probably know, I work for ISO – Insurers' Security Organization. That's funded by most of the insurance companies

62

in Britain and its remit is to deal with all aspects of security, which includes enquiring into the background of applicants who ask for unusually large policies – very discreetly carried out, of course, since one questions the honesty of the wealthy at one's peril. Maurice Rook approached the Anstey Assurance Company three years ago and requested a policy of a million pounds. Because of the amount involved, I was asked to make enquiries.

'He was born in reduced circumstances – his mother was a single parent, his father a question mark. He had a minor brush with the law when he was fifteen – a spot of vandalism – but that's the only trouble with authority. He worked for an estate agent soon after he turned seventeen and one of the people who remembers him describes him as smart, sharp, and smooth enough to persuade any woman who caught his fancy to have a look at his etchings.

'When he left that firm, he set up a partnership specializing in property development and before long gained the reputation of being one jump ahead of the competition; thanks, one person said sourly, to a lack of scruples. Presumably, he meant a greater lack than is normally found in the property field. Four years on and he was taken to court by his two partners who claimed he had been short-changing them, but their claim failed. Later, there were rumours of bribery up north where he was promoting a major development, but no case was brought. These indications of doubtful business ethics worried Anstey, but since there was no proof any of the rumours was justified, they eventually decided to issue the policy. A little after this, he retired and moved here. Payments on the policy, which naturally are considerable, have been regularly made, on time.

'You'll know as well as I that there are people who regard insurance as a financial reserve, to be called on when necessary. Running short of money? Sell a diamond ring and claim on the insurance on the grounds of loss or theft. Working as I do, one gains a "nose" for such bogus claims; it's my nose which has brought me to the island.

'I have to say from the start, there is no hard evidence this is a bogus claim. But despite lacking any proof, I'm convinced it is. There are those hints in Rook's career that he is prepared to cut corners, the absence of his body – drowning is a favourite with false claims because it's feasible the body never will be found and the insurance company can only delay presumption of death for so long – and the fact that his wife, the beneficiary, immediately informed us of his disappearance at sea.'

'She has made a claim already?'

'No. She merely advised us of his disappearance. In fact, the beneficiary is required to do so, but in the circumstances it is to some extent unusual for it to be done so quickly. One might expect her to wait since to register his disappearance so quickly suggests she believes it likely he is dead, whereas a wife normally hopes her husband will turn up safe, long after it's reasonable to hope. Obviously, even collectively these facts offer a tenuous reason for suspicion, but...'

'Your nose is certain?'

Noyes smiled.

'So how do you want to start our enquiries?'

'You don't object to my making suggestions?'

'On the contrary,' Alvarez answered, happy to escape the chore of deciding what to do.

'Ninety-nine times out of a hundred, an insurance swindle is prompted by lack of money, so a check on Rook's financial affairs might well be rewarding.'

'Then we speak to Señora Rook. She can tell us which bank her husband used. Being wealthy, he will have held as little money as possible here — one does not voluntarily assist the tax bandits — but his local bank will know from where outside Spain he drew his money. There may, naturally, be a problem persuading a bank to give us the information since there is no proof he has attempted to commit fraud, but it is likely I will know someone who works in the branch.

'It is certain he will have employed staff. We will talk to them and discover if they have, as often happens, learned more than their employers would have wished. One of the things they can tell us is, have there recently been signs of a reduced lifestyle ... Can you suggest further moves?'

'For the moment, I don't think I can. So do we start now?'

'I suppose so,' Alvarez replied, as he stared down at his empty glass.

Eight

As they drove along Vall de Mayuorka and Son Raldo came into sight, Noyes whistled. 'What a setting!'

The mountains were dramatic in form and stark of surface; in the time of the Moors, many of the lower slopes had been terraced and olive trees planted – the centuries had given them tortured shapes; the floor of the valley was gently undulating and generations of peasants had cleared the land of rocks, tilled and fertilized it, so that it had become rich and productive; only the one house, Son Raldo, was visible and this, stone built, large, gaunt and lacking any suggestion of architectural sophistication, challenged the mountains and dared them to try to crush it. A modern, Italianate villa, stylishly attractive, would have looked defenceless.

Alvarez braked the Ibiza to a stop in front of the stone steps which led up to the massive, panelled wooden door, striated by generations of weather. When he'd been young, those who lived in possessiós such as this had held such power and position that a peasant approached them with downcast eyes and bowed shoulders. Absurdly, infuriatingly, he experienced sharp nervousness as he climbed the steps and used the cast-iron knocker.

Diego opened the door, stared at Alvarez for several seconds, said, in Mallorquin: 'Don't I know you?'

'What did I arrest you for?'

'Always the joker!'

It had not been entirely a joke. In Alvarez's opinion, the appearance and behaviour of the modern generation qualified most of them for the law's attention. 'Is Señora Rook here?'

'She's down by the pool ... Is there any news of the señor?'

'None.'

'Do you think he's still alive?'

'All I can say is there's been no word of him and no body has been recovered.'

A woman stepped into the spacious, high-ceilinged hall which was furnished lightly with the simple taste that was expensive. She looked quickly at Alvarez and Noyes, then at Diego.

'Inspector Alvarez,' Diego said.

'You are policemen?' she asked in reasonable Spanish.

'I am from the Cuerpo General de Policia,' he answered. 'I apologize for troubling you, Señora Rook, but we should like to speak to you. My companion is Señor Noyes, who has flown out from England.'

She nodded at Noyes, then said: 'Señora Rook is my aunt.'

'My apologies.'

'How were you to know?' She smiled briefly.

Her smile filled her face with warmth and caused him to reassess her appearance. She was far from beautiful, but her deep brown eyes were lustrous, her retroussé nose added a touch of impishness, her lips were generous and shapely, her figure, defined with grace by a colourful frock, shapely, but not exaggerated.

'Have you learned anything?'

'I'm afraid not.'

'When you said you were a policeman, I hoped ... You want to speak to my aunt? It's obviously a very difficult time for her, so would you be as brief as possible?'

'Of course, señorita.'

'Would you like to come through?'

He followed her. She moved, Alvarez noted, with the ease of someone in good physical condition; her dress briefly tightened to each step, confirming her buttocks were well formed ... He silently swore. Did a man never overcome lascivious thoughts before he died, know no peace until the ultimate peace?

They went through a large sitting room,

furnished with expensive comfort, out to the covered patio, down the gently sloping lawn, one part of which was being sprayed by a permanent irrigation system, to the large pool lined with mosaic tiles.

Gloria lay face down on a patio chaise longue in the shade of the pool complex. On the table by her side was a cooler, in which was an opened bottle of champagne, and an empty glass. On their approach, she raised her head and looked up, then swivelled around to sit.

'Inspector Alvarez from the police and Mr Noyes from England,' Gail said.

It was true, Alvarez thought. If rich men bothered to marry, it was to exotically beautiful women considerably younger than themselves. Trophies as well as wives. Dark glasses concealed her eyes, adding a touch of mystery to a perfectly formed face framed by carefully fashioned blonde hair; her lips were full, moist, and inviting; her bikini top confirmed her breasts were pert; her waist, even as she sat, looked almost small enough to be encompassed by a man's hands; her legs were long and shapely and a man's hands...

'Have you...' she began, then abruptly stopped.

'I very much regret, señora, we have not been able to find the señor.'

'Oh, God! ... Then what are you doing

70

here?' she demanded fiercely. 'Why aren't you looking for him? He must have swum ashore, but was too injured to move any further. You have to find him.'

'I can assure you that every possible landing place on Cap Parelona has been examined.'

'It's almost a week,' she said, now speaking in little more than a whisper. 'Even if he...' She looked away.

'Do you have to upset her like this?' Gail asked sharply.

'It is very unfortunate, but the señora may be able to help us,' he answered quietly.

'How? Maurice left here soon after breakfast and that's all anyone can tell you.'

'I understand. But—'

'I think you should leave now.'

She had spoken in a tone which suggested that if they did not do so, they would be ordered out. There was, Alvarez decided, determination behind her quiet manner. 'I am only sorry we have had to be here, señorita, and we will leave, but first perhaps you will be kind enough to have a word with us?'

She stared at him for several seconds before she said: 'Up at the house.'

Alvarez and Noyes walked up to the house, stepped into the cool of the sitting room. 'I reckoned there was little point in questioning her further when she's so emotionally upset,' Alvarez said.

'That's probably right.'

'You are not certain?'

'Call me a cynic, but I'd judge her emotions to be forced.'

Could a man ever correctly judge a woman's emotions? he wondered.

Gail entered the room. 'Gloria's asked me to apologize for not offering hospitality and will I do so now. Would you like coffee or a drink?'

'A small drink would be very acceptable,' Alvarez answered.

'Please sit.' She crossed to the far wall and pressed a bell-push, returned to an armchair and sat. 'You want a word with me?'

'Yes, señorita.'

'As I said, the last time I, or anyone else, saw Maurice was when he drove off to go down to the port and sail to Mahon. So how can I possibly tell you anything?'

'Whenever there is a serious accident, we have to investigate the circumstances in order to try to make certain such a thing does not happen again.'

'But we can't have the slightest idea what happened when we were here and Maurice was miles away in his boat.'

'You can tell us how the señor was when he left here.'

The door opened and Diego entered. 'Will you say what you'd like?' she said.

72

Alvarez, in Mallorquin, asked for a coñac with ice; Noyes, in English, a coffee: Gail, in Spanish, did not want anything.

She waited until Diego had left, then said sharply: 'What exactly do you mean, how Maurice was?'

'Did he appear to be upset or depressed?'

'Just what are you getting at?'

'Señorita, this is difficult for me.'

'I'm not exactly finding it easy.'

'You must understand I regret very much having to ask such questions. But there has to be the possibility ... May I ask you not to mention to the señora what I say to you now?'

'That depends what it is.'

'It will be much kinder for her.'

She studied him, her brow creased. 'If I think it really will be kinder, naturally I'll say nothing.'

'We have to consider the possibility of suicide.'

'Good God!'

'As I have mentioned, Señor Noyes has recently arrived from England and he is here because the señor's life is insured for a very considerable sum.'

'I still don't understand.'

'Under the policy, if the señor commits suicide, it is cancelled.'

'And you're suggesting Maurice deliberately drowned himself?'

73

'I am suggesting nothing, señorita. What I am saying is that because of the terms of the insurance policy, it is necessary to establish whether there is any possibility of suicide. The señor would know his policy would be invalidated and his wife would not benefit from it if suicide was proved, so he would not write a farewell note or in any other way give an indication of what he intended. However, it is sometimes possible to judge the possibility from surrounding circumstances, such as the emotional state of the person. That is why we need to know if the señor appeared to be depressed.'

Several seconds passed before she said sharply: 'You're asking me to act the part of a spy.'

'To establish the truth.'

'Which might destroy Gloria's future.'

'A future based on a lie, señorita.'

'Isn't that being rather sanctimonious?'

'I'm afraid the law—'

'All right, you have a job to do even should you not like doing it. Just don't ask me to sympathize with you.'

The door opened and Diego entered. He handed a glass to Alvarez, put a tray, on which were cup and saucer, coffee pot, milk, and brown sugar, down on the small piecrust table at the side of Noyes's chair, left.

'I'm sorry,' Gail said as the door closed.

'For what, señorita?'

74

'For being rude, for forgetting that personal loyalties sometimes aren't all-important ... Maurice wanted an early breakfast, so I was down to see it was ready for him – the staff don't always respect time. As far as I could judge, he was his usual self. Cheerful and chatty.'

'He ate well?'

'Two eggs, two rashers of bacon, toast, marmalade, coffee. And when I gave him a packed lunch, he said the sea always made him hungry and as he wouldn't be arriving at Mahon until the late afternoon because he'd be sailing at cruising speed, would I add a couple more sandwiches.'

'Was the señora up when he left?'

'She is not an early riser.'

'Did he say goodbye to her?'

'I suppose now you're wondering if their relationship had fallen apart and that was affecting him? To repeat, he was as cheerful as ever, so of course he went up to their bedroom just before he left. Since I wasn't there, I can't swear he actually kissed her a fond goodbye.'

Alvarez drank. The brandy was of a far better quality than he enjoyed at home. It was said wealth did not make for happiness. However, it certainly helped to keep unhappiness at bay. 'I understand the señor was retired?'

'Some time ago.'

'Obviously, he was successful in business.'

'As you say, obviously.'

'So there have been no problems with money?'

'I ... I don't think so.'

'You seem doubtful?'

'Just finding it difficult to answer since I'm not conversant with their financial affairs.'

'Then we shall have to make some enquiries. The señor will have used a local bank. Which one is it?'

'I don't know I should give you that kind of personal information.'

'Then I shall have to ask the señora for the name of the bank and she will almost certainly want to know why.'

'Do you always blackmail people you're questioning?'

'I am doing no such thing...'

'All right, I apologize again for talking out of turn. It's just that when one is asked to bend one's loyalties...' She became silent.

'Señorita, there is no need to apologize. I appreciate how difficult it must be for you.'

'Do you?' She stared directly at him. 'Yes, I think perhaps you do.'

He was pleased by her words.

'It's the Banco de Costa.'

He drained his glass. 'Thank you for everything, señorita. Now, we will leave. But I should explain that at another time we will be speaking to the staff.'

'To discover if I've been telling you the truth about Maurice?'

'Señorita, I have no doubts.'

'An answer capable of ambiguity,' she said and smiled.

They said goodbye. She went with them to the front door and would have opened it had not Alvarez forestalled her.

He settled behind the wheel of the Ibiza and, as Noyes secured his seat belt, started the engine.

'There wasn't time to have a word with one or two of the staff now?' Noyes asked.

Had the English no respect whatsoever for the luncheon hour?

Nine

Noyes had agreed there was nothing to be gained by his joining Alvarez when the staff were questioned since he would understand nothing, so Alvarez was on his own when he returned to Son Raldo in the late afternoon as the shadows of the western mountains were beginning to creep across the floor of the valley.

Marta, in appearance enjoying the bloom of youth but little else, opened the front door. 'Yes?' Her manner was far from servile. She might be a maid, but as a Mallorquin, she was as good as any guest.

'I'm Inspector Alvarez, Cuerpo. I've come to have a word with—'

'The señora's not here.'

'And Señorita Rook?'

'She's out as well.'

He was sorry; he would have liked to meet her again. 'Then I'll have a word with you.'

'Why?'

He smiled. 'There's no cause for alarm. Just a few questions, the answers to which might help me.'

'I suppose you'd better come in, then.'

He followed her through to a large kitchen which appeared to have almost as much equipment as an electrical store. Luisa, plump, as so many Mallorquins became in middle age, stood at the centre table as she worked olive oil into flour with her hands; there were dabs of flour up to her elbows. She straightened up and, her hands in the bowl, stared at Alvarez.

'He's a policeman,' Marta said.

'I can tell from the look of him he's not used to work.'

Luisa, he thought, was a bulexa – an expression peculiar to Mallorca, which denoted a woman of thrusting character, ever ready to speak her mind and even contradict a man. Dolores was a bulexa, though it would take a braver man than he to call her such.

'He wants to ask questions, though I can't think why,' Marta said.

'Because he's nothing better to do.'

Alvarez decided to assert his presence. 'Perhaps we could sit down somewhere and—'

'I've time to sit when there's a meal to prepare?' Luisa worked the flour more energetically.

He was hot, tired, and his legs felt weak, but even though there was a chair beyond the table, he was not going to sit whilst she stood, affording her the chance to make further derogatory comments. 'I'm trying to understand how things were before the señor sailed away and disappeared. Did you see him that morning?'

'I made sandwiches and gave them and some cake to the señorita, then made some more sandwiches, that's all.'

'You didn't see him?'

'Isn't that what I've just said?'

'Then as far as you know, he was behaving quite normally?'

Marta giggled.

'There's no call for that,' Luisa snapped. 'You don't understand that all he does...'

'I understand perfectly.'

He spoke to Marta. 'Did you see the señor before he left here?'

'Just for a moment.'

'How was he?'

'Much the same as ever.' She giggled again.

'In what way, exactly?'

'As he said good morning, he...'

'Well?'

'Well, he ... kind of patted me.'

'Patted you?'

'Tapped me on the ... You know.'

'When I was your age,' Luisa snapped, 'I would have died rather than admit such a disgrace.'

'It was only fun.'

'And you would like me to believe you

80

don't know where a man's fun ends?'

'You can't think I would ever let him do anything.'

'I'll keep my opinion to myself.'

'You've got a nasty mind.'

'I've a mind that sees what it sees.' She picked up the plastic bottle of olive oil and squeezed more energetically than intended so that too much oil went on to the flour.

'The señor obviously likes pretty women,' he said.

Marta simpered.

Luisa looked up to face her. 'Have you finished the cleaning?'

'There's only the fourth spare bedroom to do.'

'Then you can do it now.'

'I'm going home to take my mother to the medical centre.'

'You are not leaving until—'

'The señora said it would be all right.'

'You should have spoken about it to me.'

'Why?'

'I am in charge of the housekeeping.'

'It's her says I can leave early, not you.' She turned and stamped her way out of the kitchen.

As José Gaya had written, the best way to catch a fox is to set a trap for a rabbit. 'It's difficult to understand the young of today,' Alvarez said, in disapproving tones.

Luisa walked across to the double-door

81

refrigerator. 'They've no manners.' She opened the right-hand door. 'And they've forgotten the meaning of virtue.' She brought out a glass jar.

He doubted she had ever been given the chance to forget her virtue.

'One cannot,' she continued, as she shut the door and returned to the table, 'switch on the television without seeing young girls disgustingly flaunting themselves.'

He would have liked to know which channel she was referring to. 'From what Marta said, the señor was in a happy mood.'

'Were her head not as empty as a priest's pocket, she would understand a man who thinks himself a great hidalgo, as does the señor, is friendly with the likes of her for only one reason.'

'He was often after women?'

'It is not for me to tell what happens when the señora goes away.' She emptied the jar into the bowl, worked the mixture with her hands. 'But I will say this, not a thought does he have as to the insult he gives when he calls on me to prepare food for his puta.'

'He brings women here?'

'And some are worse than putas since they are married.'

'They probably have boring husbands.'

'You understand nothing. It is not boring husbands which brings them here, it is the big house. They imagine themselves living

82

here as the señora. Of course, he knows that is what attracts them. How weak we are in the face of men's wiles!'

'Presumably, the señora is ignorant of that side of his life?'

'Then you suppose wrongly since not long ago ... You think I am the kind of person who speaks behind the backs of those who employ her?'

'Of course not.'

'Then why ask such questions?'

'It's my job.'

'No doubt you would say the swineherd is not responsible for the stink when he fails to clean out the sty?'

'The señor is very rich?'

'Does a man who lives in this house have to count his coins to find out if he can pay the bills?'

'I've known those who started wealthy, then lost much of their money and had to live like the rest of us.'

'The fool empties his pockets quickly.'

'But the señor has not emptied his?'

'If he's dead, he has no pocket.'

'True enough. But he wasn't unlucky enough to lose a fortune when the stock markets crashed?'

'How would I know about such things?'

'There'd be economies. Expensive food would not be bought, ordinary wine would be drunk, bills would not be settled quickly.'

'You think the señor paid his bills immediately? Then you know nothing of the rich. No one is closer with the euros than the man with a million.'

'It seems the señora will not starve if the señor, as seems sadly likely, is dead.'

'Her starve? You know as little about women as the rich. She will never starve all the time she can walk the streets. And how can she be poor when there is all this?' She gestured with her right hand, scattering a little flour in the air, to indicate the property.

'I suppose it must be worth a fortune these days.'

'For you and me, a fortune beyond anything we can ever know.'

'Nothing changes. When I was young, a man approached a house like this in awe.'

'But he held his head high if he was a Mallorquin,' she said fiercely.

'True. We have survived because we have never knelt to anyone – Romans, Vandals, English ... And yet,' he added slowly, 'I sometimes wonder if we have surrendered our heritage. Where are the shops which sold a pinch of this and a few grams of that as one chatted? Swept away by supermarkets which sell food from around the world instead of from this island because the foreigners demand it; which are owned and run by people with no time to chat. Where are the fields which border the sea? Under concrete.

Where are the beaches on which one could walk in solitude and find oneself? Covered with tourists.'

'Who have no shame and, like putas, flaunt their bodies.'

He recalled a recent afternoon when he had been in the port and a couple of hundred metres beyond the main beach area there had been a young and very shapely woman who had decided she wanted an over-all tan.

She said, her tone expressing her surprise: 'I would not expect to hear a policeman talk as you have just done.'

'Why not?'

'Because a policeman usually has as much thought for such things as a piece of rock.'

'Only if not born on the island ... I must have a word with Diego before I leave.'

'You'll be here a long time, then, since he's away, no doubt making a fool of himself with some woman.'

'One's only young once.'

'Which for most men is once too often ... This heat makes one thirsty.'

'Indeed it does,' he agreed with little enthusiasm, convinced she would not pursue the logic of what she had said.

'You look like a man who knows how to enjoy a coñac.'

'I sometimes think that is so.'

'Then I will pour you one to ease your

thirst.'

He hid his surprise.

'And perhaps I will give myself one as well; a small one since I have work to do.'

So did he, but he hoped she would not consider that a reason for parsimony where he was concerned.

Alvarez was about to leave the office for his merienda when the phone rang. He regarded it with dislike, finally reached forward and lifted the receiver.

'The superior chief will speak with you,' Salas's secretary said in her plum-laden voice.

He wondered, as he waited, if it had ever occurred to her that a 'Good morning' cost little effort.

'Where is it?' demanded Salas, who also eschewed social niceties.

'Where is what, señor?'

'You have no idea what I'm talking about?'

'I don't understand how I could have when—'

'You define the problem with precision. You understand very little. What I am asking you is: where is your report?'

'In connexion with what?'

'There are times when your lack of competence still surprises me. I am referring to your investigation into the missing Englishman. Did you meet Señor Noyes at the

86

airport, as I ordered?'

'Of course I met him and—'

'What day is it today?'

The change of subject was so abrupt, Alvarez failed to reply.

'Obviously, it is too much to expect you to be that aware of what goes on. Today is Wednesday. Señor Noyes arrived on Monday. How many days ago is that?'

He wondered if Salas had been drinking.

'You are as unconversant with mathematics as with so many other subjects? It is three days ago. Three days during which I have not received a single word from you to indicate what you have been doing, thereby suggesting you have been doing nothing.'

'I have been very busy—'

'Restrain your imagination.'

'I have questioned Señora Rook and a member of the staff—'

'Why only one?'

'Luisa was the only person in the house at the time ... With respect, señor, it isn't three, it's two.'

'Two what?'

'Days between today and when Señor Noyes arrived.'

'You have lost thumb, forefinger, and middle finger?'

A drunken superior chief had to be addressed even more circumspectly than a sober one.

'Well?'

'I'm afraid I can't appreciate why my fingers have anything to do with it.'

'I was suggesting that if you are unable to determine how many days, that is probably because you use your fingers in order to count and you were lacking two and a thumb.'

'I'd still have the other.'

'The other what?'

'Hand. I'd be able to use the fingers and thumb on that, wouldn't I?'

'Stop wasting my time by talking nonsense and make your report.'

'I would first like to make the point it really is two not three—'

'Are you incapable of understanding what I say?'

'I have to confess I sometimes find it a little difficult, señor.'

'Your report!'

Alvarez briefly detailed what he had done.

'Are you giving Señor Noyes all the assistance of which you are capable?'

'Yes, señor.'

'Are you making certain that expenses are minimal?'

'I'm watching every peseta.'

'Hardly reassuring when the currency has been the euro for some considerable time.'

'We Mallorquins do still tend to think in pesetas.'

'I suppose it is surprising you have the capacity to have moved on from asses.'

'We have never used animals as currency.'

'In Roman times, asses were the equivalent of four sesterces. Of course, in this island the reference does tend to gain additional relevance. Are you working satisfactorily with Señor Noyes?'

'Very much so.'

'Then he is not a demanding man. What further persons have you to question?'

'The people who work in the boatyard and anyone who might have seen Señor Rook sail off – their evidence might be relevant – and the other staff at Son Raldo. Then López can give us his opinion of whether the señora's concern at her husband's failure to arrive at Mahon seemed genuine—'

'Start questioning all those people and stop wasting my time.'

'Yes, señor. About the question of whether there were two or three days—'

The line went dead.

Alvarez replaced the receiver. In all fairness, Salas should have allowed him to point out that although Monday, Tuesday, and Wednesday did add up to three days, there had been just two working days since it was now only ten thirty in the morning. But had superior chiefs, sober or drunk, ever bothered about the facts?

He left the office for his delayed merienda.

Ten

Alvarez watched the tourists pass the window of the Club Llueso and fantasized a life in which he enjoyed full-time leisure. He picked up his glass to drink, found it was empty; about to go to the bar, he noticed the time. Officially, no officer enjoyed a coffee break; unofficially, a quarter of an hour was reasonable; he had already been away from the office for three-quarters of an hour. He stood and walked towards the outer door.

'Not thinking of leaving early, are you?' the bartender asked sarcastically.

'Some of us have to work.'

'When did you find that out?'

The old square, with one of the three village churches to the north, seemed almost as hot as proverbial hell. Sweat began to prickle his face and neck and the thick air pressed down on him as he edged his way through the throng of tourists. It was bitter to remember that but for the missing Rook, he would be on holiday, doing nothing...

'You look very grim!'

He stopped and turned to face Gail, who

90

wore a blouse and short shorts. He did not approve of women in shorts; except, that was, when they had legs as shapely as hers.

'So grim, I didn't know whether I dare greet you.'

'I'm afraid I was deep in thought.'

He was barged aside by a man and woman, arm-in-arm, who did not apologize. French, he surmised.

'Thought too serious to waste time talking to a flipperty female?' she asked, as he stepped back.

'It could never be that serious.'

'Good. But I'd better not keep you any longer.' She smiled.

'Are you in a hurry, señorita?'

'I didn't think there was such a word on this island.'

'Then may I offer you a coffee?'

'I accept with pleasure.'

Tables and chairs were set in the shade of awnings outside Club Llueso and he imagined that she would probably choose to sit at one of them. But there, they would be in full view of passers-by and there were many small-minded villagers who delighted in gossip. 'There's air-conditioning, so it'll be much cooler inside.'

'Then let's go inside.'

Remembering the strange custom foreigners observed, he held open the door for her to enter. She sat at one of the window tables.

'What would you like?' he asked.

'A cortado, please.'

'And a small coñac with it, as is the custom?'

'That would be great.'

The day sparkled as he crossed to the bar.

'I see it didn't take you long to return to work,' the bartender said. 'And I guess you'll be at it deep into the night.'

'Two cortados, two coñacs, any more comments and I'll find good reason to close this dump down.'

'Your trouble is, you've no sense of humour.'

'And yours is an inability to appreciate a man can meet a woman and not think of bed.'

'When he's not reached ninety?' The bartender turned away to prepare the coffee.

As Alvarez sat opposite Gail, she said: 'I hope you don't mind?'

'Mind what, señorita?'

'Please call me Gail. "Señorita" makes things so impersonal and I hate that.'

He wondered how, when he'd first met her, he had failed to appreciate that she might not be beautiful, but she was attractive.

'I spoke to you outside because ... I wanted to apologize for being rather rude to you the other day.'

'I don't remember anything like that.'

'That's being too kind. I also wanted...'

She stopped as the bartender came across to their table and put cups, saucers, and glasses down on it. As he left, she looked at her glass. 'That's an enormous brandy.'

Alvarez would have complained had it not been.

'I'm sure I won't be able to drink it all. Maybe you'll finish it?'

'If necessary, I will certainly try.'

She hesitated, then said quickly: 'I want to know, is there any news?'

'I'm afraid not.'

She fidgeted with her glass. 'I hope this doesn't sound terrible, but if it were certain what had happened, even were it that Maurice had drowned, it would be so much kinder. Uncertainty makes things seem even worse than they are.'

'Sadly, it always does.'

'One hopes and hopes with one part of one's mind while another part knows that if he were alive, we must have heard from him by now.' She sipped the brandy, replaced the glass on the table. 'I can't believe my uncle is dead, even while I accept he must be. I know that's being emotionally illogical, but it's so difficult to accept that someone whom you last saw alive and fit has just vanished for good.' She began to twist the glass around with her fingers, her gaze unfocused. 'It's strange how siblings can be such opposites. Father, bless him, liked life to be ordered and foreseeable, Maurice likes ... liked the excitement of chaos and never considered the future. That was why mother was so against father lending him the money. But that's all water under the bridge. Remember the good, not the bad. When father died, Maurice kindly suggested that I join them. I'd just been made redundant, hadn't any money, and was grateful. And as Gloria said, if I was worried about living off them, I could give a hand running the house ... And now, not even an optimist can really think Maurice is alive. But how can you begin to believe he might have committed suicide? When one of the screws of *Corrina* became tied up in the netting, it was typical of him to go over the side to clear it, forgetting the old sailing adage, Never leave a boat at sea without a man at the helm. Can't you understand that?'

'Of course.'

'But it's not enough because your name is Doubting Thomas ... Damn! There I go again, shouting my mouth off. You must find me very obnoxious.'

'Far from it.'

'Not when I keep insulting you?'

'I don't feel in the least bit insulted.'

'You're a kind person. It makes a tremendous difference at a time like this.' She smiled at him.

García Bocanegra had written that one

smile could cause more harm than a hundred blows. He wanted to keep her smiling, to talk about anything that would entertain her, but he was a policeman and now it was his duty, however obnoxious that was, to act hypocritically and seek information in the guise of sympathy. 'It's a very sad time for all of you and my work can only make it sadder. But, believe me, I would not willingly—'

She interrupted him. 'You don't have to say it. I know how you wish you didn't have to do what you're doing.' She reached across the table and briefly rested her hand on his in a gesture of understanding.

He drank some brandy, hoping it would help to dull his conscience. 'The señora must be very shocked.'

'Yes.'

He had not missed the suggestion of doubt. 'But she is managing to cope with things?'

'Better than I imagined she would since she can be rather emotional. In fact, I've been wondering if ... Well, if she's living in false hope.'

'She does not believe the señor has drowned?'

'If she's accepted he must have done, surely she'd be distraught? They've had their problems, but what married couple haven't? At heart, she sees him how she wants to – Prince Charming. But she's not distraught,

95

so she must have convinced herself against all the odds that he is still alive. Frankly, I've been wondering if I ought to try to make her face the truth because the vain hope must sooner or later vanish and then maybe she'll be hit even harder than acknowledging the facts now. Do you think I ought to try, or should I leave her to work things out for herself?'

'I'm sure it's impossible to give worthwhile advice, señorita ... Gail. How can one judge her reaction until the moment arrives and then it is too late to rectify a mistake.'

She tore open one of the small packs of sugar and poured the contents into her coffee. 'It's sad, but maybe also bitterly salutary, to learn how quickly life can change. Barring a few hiccups, they lived the life of dreams – a wonderful house on a wonderful island, all the luxuries anyone could possibly covet, the means to travel anywhere they wanted. But life is jealous and doesn't allow anyone to be too lucky. First there were the business problems which I'm sure is why Gloria had to sell...' She stopped abruptly. 'Why do I keep on and on remembering when I want to forget? Can you answer that?'

'It's often more difficult to forget than remember.'

'Then please ... Know something ridiculous? I have no idea what your name is.'

'Enrique.'

'Enrique, please help me forget by telling me all about the fiesta of the Moors and the Christians.'

Although not born in Llueso, he spoke with the pride of someone who had been. The Moors had made constant raids, killed villagers and taken prisoners to be held to ransom or sold into slavery. Each time a raid took place – heralded by a lookout on one of the watchtowers on top of the hill which Llueso was built on and surrounded – the villagers went to battle armed with swords, knives, staves, roasting spits and, so it was claimed, even frying pans. In May 1550, they had gained a remarkable victory and sent the Moors fleeing. This was celebrated at the beginning of each August when the villagers (men dressed in nightshirts because their ancestors had been called from their beds) struggled with the Moors (men with darkened faces and dressed as exotically as imagination decreed). Fierce blows were exchanged and a cannon with blanks was fired at irregular intervals, to the peril of Christians, Moors, and onlookers. Final victory was secured in the football ground as the last Moor fell. Subsequent celebrations were enjoyed by both living and dead and continued through most of the night, ensuring little work was done the next day.

'I'll watch it with a much more intelligent interest,' she said.

'Perhaps ... Perhaps you would like me to explain what's happening in greater detail on the day?'

'That really would be fun.'

He drank most of his brandy, poured what remained into his coffee. What had started as a morning to forget had become one to be remembered. Or remembered as he would have wished it to be. Forget he had played a duplicitous role, encouraging her under the guise of consoling chatter to provide information which could help to determine whether Rook was dead or alive and a fraudster. There were times when a man would rather not look in a mirror because of whom he would see.

Alvarez met Noyes at eight thirty that evening and suggested a meal at El Ami de Pescador, a small restaurant in the port, so apparently undistinguished that tourists looked at the dingy exterior and walked on. The interior would no more have encouraged them. Old fishing gear, dusty and disintegrating, was attached to the walls, which for some years had needed redecorating; there were no tablecloths; menus were printed only in Mallorquin and Spanish; a request for a hamburger with chips would be met with disdainful incomprehension. Yet for those who knew, if the chef was feeling in a good mood, it was a gastronomic temple.

They sat at a table behind which hung crossed harpoons. Noyes, understanding nothing in the menu, said: 'I'll have what you have and I know I'll be enjoying a royal feast.'

Alvarez wasn't certain whether that was a compliment to his taste or a comment on his waistline. 'I think you like garlic?'

'When I'm not near enough to my wife to hear her complaints.'

'We'll start with gambas al ajillo. And then...' He studied the menu and faced a familiar problem. Choose a dish and later one might wonder whether another would have proved a better choice. Truchas a la Navarra could bear the kiss of heaven, but dorada al sal could be heaven...

The waiter came to their table. Alvarez gave the order – gambas and dorada – asked for two coñacs and a bottle of Marqués de Cáceres. The brandies were quickly brought.

'You mentioned you'd met Rook's niece,' Noyes said, as he warmed the glass in his hand.

'This morning, when I had to leave the office for a spot of outside work. She had a coffee with me and because she's naturally upset, I'm certain said more than she would have done at another time. She expressed her surprise at Señora Rook's self-control and clearly would have expected her to be considerably more distressed; she thinks

Señora Rook has convinced herself, despite the evidence, that her husband is still alive.'

'You may have come up with something sharp! It's always difficult to carry out a successful scam like this one where simulated grief has to be maintained for quite a time, so when it's apparently safe, it's a relief to drop the play-acting. Mrs Rook clearly forgot her niece might inadvertently say something to us which she would consider unimportant, but we would find very interesting.'

'I also learned there was a financial problem and because of it, Señora Rook may have had to sell something ... Unfortunately, the señorita did not identify the problem or what was sold.'

'Then let's guess. In England, Rook was into property development. So if he's carried on working here, the likelihood has to be, he's interested in a development; if there's a money problem, that development has run into big trouble. The last thing someone setting up an insurance scam wants is to be seen to have financial problems, so his wife sells what to provide the cash to continue living as normal? Could be many things, but jewellery has to be in the top spot. How do we find out if my guesses are correct?'

'I will have a further word with the staff. Employers so often forget employees have ears.'

Noyes raised his glass. 'Here's hoping they have very long ones.'

When Alvarez arrived home, Jaime was watching television. He poured himself a brandy, found the ice bucket was empty except for water on the bottom, picked it up and went through to the kitchen.

'You want something?' Dolores demanded.

'Some ice.'

'You intend to drink before I serve supper?'

'But I always have—'

She interrupted him. 'I must delay the meal, then, even though it may well be ruined since you have returned late.'

'It's only just after eight—'

'It is extraordinary how a man refuses to understand a meal cannot always be adjusted to his pleasure. He arrives early and shouts, "Where is my food?" He arrives late and complains it is overcooked and dried out.'

He crossed to the refrigerator. 'It smells as if everything's just right and we'll be enjoying a delicious meal.'

She made it obvious his soft words had not diverted her annoyance. 'It may well be inedible by the time you finally decide you have drunk enough.'

'If things are that critical, serve now...'

'You will allow me to make the decisions

about a meal I have spent so many hours preparing?'

'I'm only trying to help.'

'Arriving home at a reasonable hour would have been of far more help.'

He brought out an ice tray, emptied the cubes into the bucket, began to leave the kitchen.

'I suppose it is too much trouble for someone with the need to drink as quickly as possible to place the empty tray on the draining board, rather than leave it on the table and make that wet.'

He hurriedly moved it, returned to the sitting room, where he dropped four ice cubes into his glass before he sat. He spoke in a low voice. 'What's the matter with her this time?'

'God knows,' Jaime answered. 'And probably not even He understands her – or any other woman, for that much.'

'Where are the children?'

'Having a meal with Cristina.'

'Maybe that's what's annoying her.'

'Why should it?'

He couldn't think of an answer, so he drank. His mind moved on. Tomorrow, he'd try to gain co-operation from the bank, have a word with Diego, Marta, and Luisa, to find out if any of them could identify the financial problem Rook had suffered or what his wife had had to sell. Of course, it would be simpler to put the questions to Gail, but do that and it must be obvious he had been pursuing the investigation when seemingly offering understanding and sympathy. Let that happen and she would view him with contemptuous dislike ... Those who worked at the boatyard had to be questioned. Probably none of them would be able to provide information of any use, but by questioning them he could counter any suggestion from Salas that he was not pressing the investigation with imaginative thoroughness. Which reminded him that he had not yet spoken to López...

'What's up?' Jaime asked. 'You've been sitting there like a stuffed dummy for the last ten minutes.'

'You have to ask why he is silent?' Dolores said, as she came through the bead curtain, an earthenware cooking pot in her gloved hands. She came to a stop. 'I thought I asked you to put the board on the table. Of course, I have to ask for so many things to be done, perhaps I am mistaken.'

Jaime hurriedly brought out of the sideboard the circle of olive wood, still with bark, on which hot dishes were placed. He set this on the table.

She put the pot down on the wood. 'I see you have not yet been able to find the time to lay the table.'

'I was just about to do that,' Jaime said

quickly.

'Life is filled with things a man is about to do. If he drank less, perhaps he would manage to complete at least some of them.'

Jaime pointed at his glass. 'That's my first.'

'As my mother so often said, a man's imagination can weave moonbeams.'

'That is my first drink of the evening.'

'The one before that was your last drink of the afternoon?' She returned into the kitchen.

'Why won't she believe me?' Jaime asked plaintively.

'Experience.'

'Bloody funny! What's made you so sour?'

'You have to ask?' came a call from the kitchen.

Alvarez finished his drink, poured himself another. The indication was that he was responsible for Dolores's ill humour. Still, that rich smell in the kitchen meant her cooking had not been affected by her emotional state, as could happen.

She returned, having removed her apron, plates in one hand, large serving spoon in the other. 'There is the dish of rice on the cooker,' she said, as she put the plates and spoon down. When no one moved, she sighed. 'A man will run towards the sound of a cork being pulled, stumble if asked to carry out an empty bottle.' She went back into the kitchen, returned with a second earthenware

104

bowl. She spooned rice on to the first plate, lifted the lid of the larger bowl, enabling Alvarez to identify the contents. They were about to enjoy one of the dishes which, easy to prepare, difficult to prepare well, separated the brilliant cook from the good one. Arroz con ossobuco. There were those who decried oxtail as peasants' food. There were those who believed the world to be flat.

'I met Eloísa this afternoon.' She put meat and gravy on the rice, passed the plate to Alvarez.

She had looked at him as she spoke and her tone had been sharp. He tried to remember if he had recently upset Eloísa – very easily done – but became certain he had not met her in weeks.

'It was obvious she had something she wanted to tell me because she knew I would not want to hear it.' She passed a plate to Jaime.

'I can't think why you talk to the bitch,' he said.

'I will not have that language in this house even when the children are away.'

'But she's always blacking people. If I'd been you, I'd have said a quick hullo and hurried on.'

'And given her the opportunity to call me rude and snobbish?'

'If you want my opinion, you wanted to hear what she had to say.'

'What's that?'

'All I meant was—'

'Women should be grateful how rarely men mean what they say.'

'Since she obviously wanted to tell you something, you were only willing to listen out of politeness. That's all I meant.'

'Of course, they also seldom say what they mean. You would agree with that?'

'I don't understand what you're getting at.'

'Then your words were meaningless.' She served herself. 'The meat is probably tough and the rice overcooked, but there is nothing else to eat.' She sat.

'It's perfect,' Alvarez hastened to assure her. 'Another of your miracles of cooking.'

'You think it a miracle if I cook something which is edible?'

He emptied his glass, refilled it, pushed the bottle of Sangre de Toro across to Jaime. There were times when words became impotent.

'I met Eloísa,' she said again.

Jaime had half refilled his glass, saw she was not watching, filled it.

'She asked me how the family was. Then mentioned she had seen Enrique this morning.'

'Thankfully, I didn't see her,' Alvarez said.

'That is hardly to be wondered at.' She sighed.

He suddenly realized what was annoying

her. 'If Eloísa was trying to suggest some-thing because I was having coffee with a woman, she was being even more bitchy than usual.'

'She said you were not seated outside with everyone else.'

Because he had been trying, and failed, to hide from the gossips. 'Gail wanted to be cool.'

'And you'd have preferred her to be hot.' Jaime sniggered.

'You were sitting at a table,' Dolores said.

'What else does one do at a table?'

'She is a foreigner?'

'Surely Eloísa was born in Manacor?'

'It amuses you to mock me? Is this woman a foreigner?'

'She is English.'

'And very young.'

'Younger than Eloísa, but that is hardly difficult.'

'And beautiful.'

'Better looking than Eloísa, but once again, that's easy.'

'Aiyee! But life becomes an ever greater burden when age gives a woman wisdom, a man, still more stupidity.' She pushed her plate away. 'How can I eat when my heart is breaking?'

'You'd find it far less fragile if you'd listen to me, not her. I'm investigating a case which concerns a missing Englishman and Gail is his niece. I was walking through the old square when I met her and because she, naturally, is very shocked by her uncle's disappearance, I felt it would be kind to ask if she'd like a coffee.'

'A man's sympathies grow stronger as a woman grows younger.'

'Gail is younger than me, but far from beautiful. Many people would describe her as rather plain.'

'The ageing cockerel learns he has to run after hens he can catch.'

'Why won't you understand a man can talk to a woman without any ulterior motive?'

'Because I am not five years old.' She drew her plate back and began to eat.

Later, when Dolores was in the kitchen, washing up, Jaime poured himself a large brandy. 'What's this Gail really like?'

'Blonde,' Alvarez answered. 'With a face to make your heart beat a hundred times a minute, and a body to raise your temperature to fifty.'

'Why should you have all the luck?' Jaime asked sourly.

Eleven

Perez phoned at nine twenty on Thursday morning. 'Is that you, Enrique?'

He recognized the voice. 'What can you tell me about the account?'

'What's the second christian name of your cousin's daughter?'

'Why d'you want to know that?'

'To make certain you are you.'

'If I'm not me, who the hell am I? Have you been celebrating too generously?'

'If anyone ever learns what I'm doing...' Perez became silent.

'Right now, all you're doing is sounding paranoic.'

'You've got to tell me the christian name of Dolores's daughter.'

Alvarez thought, but as could happen when a mind was called upon to work very quickly, it blanked. 'Look, I can't remember right now...'

'Then I'm ringing off.'

'Hang on. It's Beatriz ... Isabel Beatriz.'

'Why did it take you so long?'

'Because she's never called Beatriz. Stop

playing double O seven and tell me what you've learned.'

'He regularly drew on a bank in another country and paid the money in to us. That is, he did until a cheque was returned because there were not enough funds to meet it.'

'Give me the date of the bounced cheque.'

'No.'

'The name of the foreign bank, then.'

'I daren't take the risk. If you start making enquiries, it could become obvious someone's been passing on information.'

It was, Alvarez thought with annoyance, unusual for a Mallorquin to be reluctant to break rules and regulations. 'Then I may have to get back on to you.'

'I'd much rather you didn't.' Perez rang off.

Alvarez leaned back in the chair. The facts were gradually becoming clear. Before long, they could be certain beyond any reasonable doubt that Rook was still alive, believing his insurance scam was succeeding.

The clerk behind the reception desk at the hotel said Señor Noyes had left not long before and, since he'd been carrying a towel, was almost certain to be on the beach. Alvarez left the hotel, crossed the road, stepped over the low wall on to the sand and visually searched the beach. There were fewer bare breasts than would have been visible four or five years before, presumably because of health warnings; since most sunbathers were foreigners, it was unlikely to have been modesty which motivated them. Noyes was seated at a circular table through the centre of which was a pole supporting a Tahiti rush sun cover.

'Have you come for a swim?' Noyes asked as Alvarez, sweating and breathing quickly because it was not easy to walk on sand, came to a stop.

'I don't think so.' Swimming was a demanding exercise.

'Then will you have a drink?'

'If you insist.'

Noyes signalled to a waiter, who came across and took the order for a coñac with ice.

Alvarez settled on the second chair within the shade. 'The forecast is that the temperature is going to rise.'

'As has been said before in two words, impossible.'

'It may reach forty or forty-one.'

'I rang Judy last night. She said it was raining and the wind was quite cold. I hadn't the heart to tell her there has hardly been a cloud since I arrived and the sea is like a warm bath ... Enough of my pleasures, what about yours?'

'I think we are perhaps a little nearer to unmasking Maurice Rook.'

111

'What have you learned?'

'I have spoken to an acquaintance who works in a bank. Señor Rook has been drawing money from abroad, but recently one of his cheques was not met because of the lack of funds.'

'The smoking gun?'

'I don't yet know the name of the bank or even which country it's in, but it should not be difficult to find out.'

The waiter returned with a brandy for Alvarez, another daiquiri for Noyes; he spiked the bill, hurried away.

'I will return to Son Raldo and speak to the staff to learn what more they know.' Alvarez raised his glass, drank. 'You might like to come with me this time?'

'I doubt there's much point to that. I won't understand a word they say unless you speak in Spanish rather than Mallorquin, and even then I'll miss most of what goes on unless you translate, which will slow things down and give them time to think about what they're going to say. Logically, it makes more sense if I stay here.'

'Much to your regret?'

'Of course.'

'I will also question Jorge Fiol, who owns the boatyard, and the men who work for him. And perhaps have a word with Andrés López.'

'I hope that leaves you enough time to have

dinner with me?'

'I have been told many times by my superior that good policing is all about priorities.'

Marta opened the right-hand front door of Son Raldo. 'You again!'

'As you say,' Alvarez agreed. 'Is the señora here?'

'She's in Palma.'

'And the señorita?'

'Left half an hour ago.'

'To go where?'

'How would I know?'

How indeed? He was annoyed at himself for having asked the question. If she was meeting a boyfriend, that was her privilege. And he was a lucky bastard. 'Then I'll have a word with you, Luisa, and Diego.'

'Not more questions?'

'Dozens more.'

She sighed.

'So if we can go through to a room.' He stepped into the hall, saw his reflection in a mirror and decided he was looking old and tired. No, just tired.

'I must tell Luisa what's happening or she'll start shouting at me for not doing my work. She's a slave driver.'

One had only to look at her to know that.

'The way she goes on, you'd think it was her money what pays me, not his ... You being here to ask more questions means you

113

still don't know anything?'

'Unfortunately, that's right.'

'Who's going to be paying us now?'

'If the señora continues to live here, she will. A house this size must have staff.'

'If it's just her, it'll be grim. He was always friendly, but she can't talk to us like we're human. I'll go and work in a hotel. They would pay me better.'

'And work you harder.'

'Than she does?' She spoke derisively.

'Suppose we go somewhere comfortable for a talk?'

She led the way into the library, on two walls of which were leather-bound books which looked as if they were seldom, if ever, read. There was an air-conditioning unit on the wall to the right of the window and she used the remote control to switch this on before she left. The fan in the outside unit started and almost immediately cold air was blown into the room.

Marta returned. 'Luisa says you're not to keep me for long.'

'What's her worry? What we could be getting up to?'

'With you?'

Was her scornful rejection because he was a policeman? Or because youth couldn't recognize the value of maturity? 'You'd best sit,' he said sharply.

She looked at him uneasily, settled in one

of the comfortable chairs.

'Tell me what it's like working here.'

She initially had some difficulty in expressing herself, but soon spoke freely. The señor was cheerful and friendly, the señora seemed to think she was the Duchess of Llueso. The señor would try to speak to them in Spanish and laugh when he made a mistake, the señora almost always spoke in English and became annoyed if they could not understand her. There was plenty of work to do because it was such a large house, there were often people staying, and there were frequent parties with dozens of guests. Still, if it weren't for Luisa, it would be a good job. Luisa was a real slave driver. Never content, always looking for something she could criticize. If there was a little dust where no one was likely to look, what did it matter?

'When I was here before,' he said, 'you gave me the impression the señor had wandering hands.'

She spoke coquettishly. Some men liked to pat a woman's bottom and where was the harm in that when it was just being friendly? Of course, Luisa thought stupid things; she'd even accused her of encouraging the señor in the hope he'd get rid of the señora and marry her. Luisa's trouble was, no man had ever tried to pat her bottom, even though there was more than enough to pat.

'The señor enjoyed female company?'

'Of course he did. With his money and being handsome, they were always after him. The señora was on guard, but when she went away on one of her trips...' She stopped.

'He didn't have lonely nights?'

'And didn't worry about us knowing. You should hear what Luisa has to say about that.'

'I have.'

She giggled. 'She's only insulted because no one's ever after her.'

'The señora never knew what was going on?'

'She did once. She was meant to be away for several days, but something happened and she was back early.'

'He and his latest were enjoying themselves?'

'Can't rightly say, but from the way the señora carried on, if they weren't at it, that was because they needed a rest.'

'There was a row?'

'My mum and dad have their arguments, same as everyone, but nothing like the señora telling the señor what she thought.'

'Do you know who this woman was?'

'She's been here several times, but only comes in the morning. I said to Luisa, that's because she's married and has to get her husband his lunch. Luisa tried to tell me I was being stupid and not even a married

116

foreigner would behave like that, but once the woman forgot to remove her wedding ring.'

'Can you give me her name?'

'Sarah.'

'Sarah what?'

She shrugged her shoulders.

'Do you know where she lives?'

'Down in the port.'

'Whereabouts in the port?'

She shrugged her shoulders again.

'Can you tell me anything more about her?'

'Not really.'

'Whoever she is, it seems the señor persuaded the señora to forgive and forget.'

'The señora's a bitch, but she knows if she creates too much trouble, he'll tell her to walk. I mean, with his money, he can easily find someone else ... Oh!'

'What's the problem?'

'I've been talking like he's still around, only he isn't, is he?'

'We can't be certain, but it seems very unlikely he is still alive.'

'The thing is ... I keep thinking he is.'

'Have you a reason for this?'

'It's just that working in the house with everything the same, it seems like he's just gone away for a while.'

'The señora's behaviour hasn't constantly reminded you that's not what's happened?'

She was perplexed by the question.

'She must be very distraught? Crying some of the time, that sort of thing?'

'I suppose so,' she answered uncertainly.

Gail was not the only person in the house to be surprised by Gloria's lack of emotion in the face of the apparent death of her husband. 'Would you know what it was the señor sold shortly before his disappearance?'

'Didn't know he'd sold anything.'

'And the señora, did she?'

'I can't say.'

'She hasn't got rid of any of her jewellery?'

After a moment, she said: 'It's funny you mentioning that.'

'Why so?'

'She used to wear enough jewels to buy a house, but recently all she's had on is her wedding ring. Her engagement ring had a diamond so big I wondered if it was real.'

'You are very observant.' The small compliment pleased her. 'That's about all I need to ask, so will you tell Diego to come and have a word?'

She left. Diego came in and answered the initial questions hesitantly. Remembering past peccadilloes? Even the honest man found reason to become nervous when facing the law.

After several minutes, Alvarez said: 'I'm trying to understand the state of the señor's mind immediately before his disappearance.

How would you describe that?'

'Didn't really notice.'

Always far more concerned with himself than other people. 'He didn't seem particularly worried? I'm interested because I've been told he ran into a whole load of trouble.'

'It didn't seem to bother him as much as it did her.'

'Why do you say that?'

'There was the time when you could hear her shouting at him and saying his cojones were bigger than his brain.'

'Woman problems?'

'Not that time.'

'Then what upset her?'

'Something about money.'

'Perhaps it had to do with the development project which had gone sour?'

'Could have been, I suppose. Come to think about it, she was shouting after he got that phone call from the lawyer in Maracena.'

'Tell me about it.'

'I wasn't trying to listen.'

'Of course you weren't.'

'It's just one hears things by mistake.'

'Very true. So tell me what you heard by mistake.'

The señor's Spanish was poor, but partially understandable. He had been very excited, telling the lawyer the land was his and the building must go ahead. The señora had been out at the time, but when she'd returned, he'd met her in the hall and spoken quickly and excitedly in English. Diego thought he'd told her that unless the lawyers could do something, they were ruined.

'I can't tell you any more than that,' Diego said.

'Then thanks for your help. And you can let Luisa know there's no need for me to bother her at the moment.'

Diego accompanied him to the front door and opened the right-hand side. As Alvarez stepped out on to the drive, a nearly new BMW braked to a halt by the side of his ancient and battered Ibiza. The window of the driving door slid down.

'What are you doing here?' Gloria demanded angrily.

'I have been having a word with two of the staff, señora.'

'Who the hell do you think you are—' She came to a sudden stop. She spoke in a low voice. 'Have you any news?'

Her initial anger had been fuelled by fear, then she'd realized that a wife whose husband was missing would show anxiety, not anger. 'I'm afraid not, señora.' He looked past her at Gail, in the front passenger seat. Gail nodded a hullo.

'I thought seeing you ... I was so hoping ... That's why I must have sounded ... Oh,

God, the uncertainty is killing me.'

The sharp sunshine, cutting across the edge of the roof of the car, was not friendly, highlighting as it did the lines in Gloria's face, but she looked robustly healthy and far from dying.

'We just have to go on hoping.' She gripped the steering wheel with both hands and stared through the windscreen, her expression taut.

Noyes, Alvarez thought, had been unkind in describing her acting ability as poor. He would describe it as reasonably good.

'Why are you here?' Gail asked.

'As I mentioned, I wanted to have a word with the staff. I'm afraid I haven't learned anything which might help the señora.'

'You expected any of them to be able to?'

'In a case like this, every possibility is worth checking.'

Gloria, her voice high, said: 'I can't sit here and listen and hope ... and hope that ... Put the car away, Gail.' She opened the driving door, stepped out, walked rapidly to the front door, held open by Diego.

Gail stepped out of the car and came round the bonnet. 'I'd better put this in the garage, as politely requested. Do you have to rush anywhere?'

'I try never to rush anywhere.'

'Then let me return your hospitality and come in and have a drink.'

'It will not disturb the señora?'

'Possibly. Hop into the car and we'll go round to the garage.'

He sat in the front passenger seat as she settled behind the wheel. She drove around the corner of the house and into a stone barn. As she switched off the engine, she said: 'There are rooms above us which look like prison cells. Diego says that in the old days, the estate workers lived in them. Can that be true?'

'Almost certainly, yes.'

'But they're so small and dark and there's no sign of anywhere to wash.'

'Many landowners used not to trouble themselves much about the conditions in which their workers lived. But other countries have also had their dark days.'

'Of course. Do you realize you spoke quite fiercely?'

'I'm sorry.'

'For heaven's sake, don't be. You're very proud of being Mallorquin, aren't you?'

'I am.'

'And you resent the foreigners who come here and sneer at anything they find odd?'

'It is difficult to appreciate other people's history.'

'Don't evade the question. You resent their patronizing stupidity, don't you?'

'I suppose sometimes I do, yes.'

'Good.'

He followed her out of the barn and across the paved yard to a side door. Beyond was a long passage which ended in the hall. 'Go up the stairs, turn right and it's the second room on the right. I'm just going to have a word with Gloria.'

He walked over to the staircase, which, like the rest of the house, lacked any grace, but possessed an air of permanence because of the stonework. As he climbed the stairs, he recalled days when it would have been absurd to suggest he would ever be a guest in such a mansion.

The room he entered was large, cool thanks to the thick walls, and furnished lightly, with the taste found elsewhere. He crossed to the window, undid and opened the shutters and swung them back to engage in their clips, stared down at the garden – a modern invention. In the old days, there would have been trees, shrubs, cacti, and weeds, not lawn, a pergola covered with roses, and flower beds bereft of any weed. Beyond the garden were small groves of orange and lemon trees, a dozen almond trees, and four ancient fig trees, their large, irregular leaves concealing branches which in winter would look like dead men's fingers. To own such a property as this was to walk with the gods. Yet as Rook must learn, the gods punished hubris...

'A penny for them,' Gail said.

123

Startled, he swung round to see her standing in the doorway.

'You looked as if you were miles away.'

'I suppose I was.'

'So where were you?'

'Just day-dreaming.'

'You're not going to say? You think a lot, Enrique. Do you remember what Caesar said of men who thought too much? They're dangerous. Perhaps you are dangerous even though you are such a nice person.'

He was warmed and chilled by her words. How would she describe him if she knew he was seeking proof of her uncle's fraud?

'Now, what would you like to drink?'

'Do you have some coñac, with just ice?'

'Coñac Español or cognac?'

A polite guest made only modest requests; temptation so often overcame politeness. 'A little French cognac would be a great treat.'

'Only a little? I remember the brandies at Club Llueso were more than generous.' She smiled. 'Will you leave me to decide the measure?'

'With pleasure.'

'And perhaps some doubt? One of Maurice's favourite complaints is no woman pours a decent drink because...' She stopped abruptly; a moment later, she said: 'Tell me something, Enrique. Is it strange that some of the time I think of Maurice as if he hadn't disappeared? Logically I know the chances of his being alive are almost nil, but emotionally I sometimes seem unable to accept that. Which is what Gloria is doing all the time and I criticize her for it.'

'There's nothing unusual about your feelings. Marta said the same thing to me earlier.'

'Before we returned, you talked to the staff. Were you able to learn anything? I know you told Gloria you'd learned nothing, but I did wonder if that was something of a fudge?'

'Nothing that could help her.' Which was true. What he had learned could not help Gloria, but would probably hurt her.

'It's a worrying, sad time. Maurice has given me a home ... I'll go and get the drinks. And when I come back, talk to me about anything but Maurice's disappearance.'

He watched her leave the room and once again noted that her athletic stride drew her skirt tight across her buttocks ... He was damned. Doomed to suffer prurient thoughts whenever they should be pure. Had she ever provided the slightest reason for his envisaging the form beneath her clothes? No. His mind was diseased. Disease had to be cured. As soon as possible, he would, forgoing a normal holiday, enter a retreat. There was no greater benefit than to suffer for one's evil. By existing on bread and water, denied alcohol and cigarettes, a man could eventually find the person he should be.

She returned. She put one glass down on the small table by the side of her chair, crossed the floor and leaned over to hand him a well-filled balloon glass. The neckline of her dress was quite low and was ballooning. He observed she was not wearing a brassière.

'I hope you approve of my measure?'

For one wild moment, he thought... 'It's perfect,' he answered, staring fixedly at the glass as he hoped it was not true that a woman could often judge where a man's thoughts lay.

She sat, raised her glass. 'To us and our future.'

Did her words suggest the development of a relationship...? He was a primitive fool. So foolish that if she said it would rain tomorrow, he would manage to interpret her words as an invitation. He was beyond hope. A year in retreat would be insufficient to cleanse his soul.

'Enrique, I regard you as the font of all information concerning the island. So you can tell me about talayots. The other day I was near Oña and stopped to look at the talayotic village there, hoping there'd be something or someone to tell me about it, but there was not a single word of information and no one. So now, professor, a history of the period.'

He sipped the cognac – possessed of a quality he very seldom enjoyed – as he struggled to remember something, anything, about the people who, six thousand years BC, had been driven from France by poverty and hunger to seek the Elysian island so richly productive that a man could choose what to eat.

Twelve

'Ignacio has died,' Dolores said, as she passed a plate.

Alvarez took the plate and put it down in front of him. Tonyina amb safrà. Tuna steak cooked with garlic, onion, egg yolk, olive oil, white wine, pine nuts, parsley, bay, saffron, pepper and salt. A dish undoubtedly served on Olympus.

'Is anyone bothering to listen to me?'

Both he and Jaime assured her they were listening to every word she said.

'It was very sudden.'

Alvarez ate the first forkful. Anticipation, especially where food was concerned, often proved to be a traitor, but not this time.

'He was at the medical centre because he wasn't feeling well and collapsed.'

'He was always a thoughtful bloke,' Jaime said.

'What is that supposed to mean?'

'Dying at the medical centre saved having to call a doctor to his home.'

'You regard death as a matter for jest?'

'Of course not—'

'No doubt you would regard my death as a time for great merriment? You could invite your dissolute friends to drink to your good luck.'

'I say something and you twist it around until I don't know what I did say.'

'If you ever stopped to think before you spoke, you might find that your memory improved.'

Alvarez and Jaime – Isabel and Juan were out – ate, nervously uncertain what her aggression presaged.

'Is it too much to hope you appreciate the significance of what I have been saying?'

Since she was staring at him, Jaime decided he had to answer. 'Ignacio is no longer alive.'

'Aiyee! I am honoured above many women. I live with a husband who occasionally decides to listen to what I say!'

He drained his glass, reached across the table for the bottle of René Barbier.

'You have drunk enough,' she snapped.

For once, he tried to show some defiance. 'I'll drink as much as I want.'

'Then I will cook as little as I wish since there is no pleasure to be gained from slaving in a kitchen, hotter than the fires of hell, preparing a meal for someone who has drunk until he does not know whether he is eating greixonera de xot or last week's leftover chicken.'

Jaime let go of the bottle.

She ate another mouthful. 'Eva is now on her own with two children to bring up.'

'Then she is not on her own,' Jaime observed.

Alvarez wondered how Jaime could have been married for many years, yet never understood that silence was not only golden, there were times when it was essential.

'So now it pleases you to jest about Eva's misery?' she said.

'All I was pointing out was—'

'Were she to discover she is suffering from a fatal disease, your mirth would undoubtedly be unchecked.'

'You'd have a saint swearing. Suppose I tell you I'm damned sorry for her—'

'I will assume you have drunk more than usual.'

There was a silence which lasted until Dolores ate the last piece of fish on her plate and put down knife and fork. 'Ignacio's uncle left him a finca a few years ago. Somewhere between here and Playa Neuva.'

'A couple of kilometres along the old road,' Alvarez said.

'You know it?'

'Old Armando boasted about the crops it grew right up to the day he died and it passed to Ignacio.'

'Then it is good land?'

'Very productive. That family have always

been good farmers and sufficiently forward looking to try new systems of land management.'

'Eva wanted to move there when Ignacio inherited it, but, being a man, he took no notice of her wishes. Now, she can sell the house in the village and use the money to restore the finca. With the foreigners paying ridiculous prices, there will be enough to make certain it becomes as grand as anywhere. Of course, she cannot work the land on her own.'

Alvarez realized the reason for the conversation. He refilled his glass.

'It will become a very comfortable home.'

'With two kids?' he said.

'A man could still do far worse for himself than marry her.'

'How?'

'What sort of a ridiculous question is that? In church, of course, since she is a widow and may marry there after a decent period of mourning.'

'I was asking, how can one do much worse than marry her? Ignacio always said she had the devil of a temper.'

'Only a woman who has the soul of an angel can live at peace with the stupidity of a man.'

Aware that he was pursuing a course for which he had silently condemned Jaime not long before, Alvarez said: 'Then, as you've just pointed out, she is no angel.'

'I have said no such thing.'

'If she has a temper—'

Dolores stood. 'I have far too much work to do to sit and listen to nonsense. Pass your plates.'

She carried them out to the kitchen, returned with a bowl in which were oranges, apples, pears, and bananas, and three clean plates. She sat, chose an apple, peeled it with unnecessary vigour. 'As my mother often had occasion to say, a woman values what she has, a man only what he has not.' She raised a quarter of apple to her mouth, sharply bit off a piece, chewed vigorously. She swallowed. 'There is no need to ask why you speak as a man devoid of his wits,' she said, staring at Alvarez.

He gave all his attention to peeling a banana.

'It has happened so often before.' She spoke with angry sorrow. 'You pursue a foreign woman half your age, too blinded by lust to understand she speaks kindly to you only because she respects the old.'

'I am not lusting after a foreign woman—'

'Did not Eloísa see you with one in Club Llueso? You wish to call her a liar?'

'Probably. And a woman who sees lust everywhere because she's not getting any.'

'Sweet Mary, never before have I heard such infamous words!'

'What's more, Gail is considerably more than half my age and the only time I see her is when I have to because of work. And I am not an old man.' He ate his banana with as much venom as Dolores ate the rest of her apple.

'You're becoming a fixture,' Fiol said, as he sat behind his large desk.

'There's no need to panic and bring out your second set of books,' Alvarez replied. 'I'm not interested in how you're fiddling your tax figures.'

'Very humorous! Why are you here?'

'To have a word with your workers.'

'Why?'

'Someone may have seen Señor Rook sail off on the day he disappeared.'

'You can find that out after work finishes.'

'It's more convenient now.'

'Convenient for who?'

'Me.'

'Doesn't matter interrupting work, does it? You only ever think of yourself.'

'That's how I stay young and cheerful.'

'Cheerful? You always look like you've lost the winning lottery ticket ... Can't you make it some other time?'

'No.'

Fiol stood.

'You're joining me?'

'Got to make certain you don't pinch anything.'

They left the office and went down the wooden steps to ground level. The noise of sanders was briefly drowned by a clash of metal and a shout. Fiol swore, hurried off.

Alvarez stared at the many boats under repair and wondered how much capital they represented, marvelled that there were those who could spend a fortune on pleasure.

Fiol returned. 'The bloody fool dropped a load of bottlescrews.'

'And broke them? How many weeks' wages are you going to overcharge him?'

'A bottlescrew doesn't break when it's dropped.'

'That won't stop you docking his wages ... That llaüt which has been in some sort of collision looks very out of place amongst all these gin palaces.'

'It wouldn't be there if I hadn't been so soft-hearted.'

'Who's enjoying the benefit of the miracle?'

'Carlos Riera.'

'Then why the collision? I always thought he was as sharp with a boat as his father was.'

'It wasn't his fault, it was Señor Rook's, who knew as much about boat handling as a stoker in the Swiss navy.'

'Carlos must have had something to say!'

'Went on and on about how he'd teach the

bastard the rich can't always get away with everything.'

'Still it's a poor summer which doesn't leave someone the richer. His incompetence has provided you with more work.'

'Which no one's paying for. The señor refused to accept responsibility, Carlos hasn't damage insurance and can't even afford to pay for the work already done, let alone what needs doing before the boat can go back to sea.'

'Which leaves him unable to earn a living. Finish the work and let him pay you back as and when he can. Better still, add a little extra to other people's bills. Someone who can afford a craft like that –' Alvarez gestured at a fifteen-metre trawler yacht – 'isn't going to notice.'

'The richer they are, the more they argue over every euro.'

'Carlos didn't think of taking the señor to court?'

'Carlos has céntimos in his pocket, the señor had five-hundred-euro notes.'

'Money doesn't buy justice.'

'Which world do you live in?'

Fiol led the way to where two men were replacing an area of fibreglass in the hull of a small yacht. 'The inspector wants a word with you,' he said. 'Keep it short.'

The questions were soon asked and answered. They both knew Rook by sight, neither had seen him the day he had sailed off to oblivion. Four more men had given the same negative evidence before Alvarez and Fiol reached a catamaran, bright blue, at which a single man, stripped to the waist, broad of shoulder, worked on one of the hulls.

'Inspector Alvarez,' Fiol said. 'Wants a word with you.'

Zapata looked at Alvarez for several seconds, then grinned, showing uneven, gappy teeth.

'Did you see Señor Rook sail off the day he disappeared?' Alvarez asked.

Zapata's grin broadened.

'Well, did you?'

'I helped him.'

'Helped him do what?'

'Carry it.'

'Carry what?'

'Carry it.'

'What the hell are you talking about?'

Fiol spoke in a low voice. 'Take it easy. He's Natalia's boy.'

Alvarez was annoyed with himself for having shown impatience. Natalia had become pregnant whilst unmarried, before that had become fashionable. Her sanctimonious parents had not thrown her out of their home, but had forbidden her to parade her shame before the villagers. Since she had had to work, when born Miguel had been in

136

the grandparents' care for most of the day. They believed evil had to be forced out of a child, so they had beaten Miguel whenever he did anything they considered to be wrong. Neighbours had probably known the child suffered, but were reluctant to denounce them and bring shame on a God-fearing couple merely because of a little bastard. One day, the beating had been sufficiently severe to inflict brain damage.

When Alvarez next spoke, his tone was quiet and friendly. 'Tell me what you carried.'

It took several minutes, and several repetitions to understand that what Zapata was talking about had taken place some time before Rook's disappearance. About to cut him short, Alvarez checked the words as he realized he was hearing unexpected evidence. Rook had parked his car near *Corrina* and by chance, Zapata had been on his way to work. Rook had been struggling to lift a large cardboard container out of the back of the BMW, so Zapata had hurried to give a hand. Even for the two of them, it had proved to be a difficult task to carry the container up the narrow gangplank and aboard ... *Corrina* was a wonderful boat; the accommodation was like a palace...

'You carried the package aboard. What happened then?'

As he stepped down on to the afterdeck,

Rook had lost his footing. The container had fallen sideways and a stanchion had torn it to reveal a small, factory-packed inflatable.

'Was the señor annoyed?'

He had been so furious, Zapata had feared he was about to be attacked. He wasn't used to foreigners behaving so aggressively. They were usually kinder than the Mallorquins, who so often laughed at him. He liked helping the foreigners because they smiled their thanks and sometimes gave him something...

'Was the inflatable damaged?'

It was only the container that had torn. After he'd returned ashore, he'd gone for his merienda and had had two ensaimadas instead of one because of the five euros he'd been given...

'The señor asked you not to mention what had happened?'

Zapata was so surprised, his mouth opened wide revealing his teeth to be even more irregular than was normally apparent. How could the inspector possibly know that?

'Did the señor explain why he'd bought a small inflatable when the boat's tender was a large one?'

The señor had said it was a surprise present for the son of a friend. What a lucky boy the son was to receive a surprise present! Only the lovely lady ever gave him anything but blows or curses. Whenever she saw him, she asked about his headaches and gave him a present.

'You've been a great help,' Alvarez said.

Zapata was delighted by the praise.

As Fiol and Alvarez walked back the length of the shed, Fiol said: 'He came asking for a job and I took him on because I couldn't help feeling sorry for him.'

'And there was I thinking it was probably because he'd work for less than anyone else.'

'You're a cynical bastard.'

They came to a halt by the steps leading up to the office. 'Did the señor entertain women aboard his boat?' Alvarez asked.

'What d'you think? There's not an aphrodisiac on the market half as effective as a couple of hours on the water.'

'Is that fact?'

'Got you thinking about buying a boat? You'd need one the size of the *Queen Mary* to do you any good.' He gripped the handrail, put his right foot on the first step.

'Hang on.'

'You've made me waste enough time.'

'The señor had women on his boat. Was that when his wife wasn't with him?'

'Why would he want her around, criticizing?'

'Do you know any of his women?'

'Do I look that lucky?'

'Can you give me some names?'

'Not unless I have to.'

'Why not?'

'Why should I spoil some poor sod of a husband's life?'

'One of them was married?'

'You're quick.'

'There may be no real need to find out who she is, so for the moment I'll forget her.'

'You wouldn't if you'd ever seen her. You'd be begging me to lend you a boat.'

Alvarez and Noyes met in Restaurante El Coq on the front at Puerta Neuva and sat at one of the outside tables, protected from the sun by an overhead awning. A waiter took their initial order for a Cinzano and a brandy.

'So what's the important news?' Noyes asked.

'Rook took a small inflatable aboard his boat some time before he disappeared.'

'Did he, by God! So that's why the tender was fast in its davits. How did you learn that?'

Alvarez recounted his meeting with Zapata at the boatyard.

'Then now we can be virtually certain. Rook has carried out an insurance scam, having run into financial problems which threatened to bankrupt him.'

'There is a problem.'

'When isn't there?'

The waiter served their drinks, asked if they were ready to order their meal, left when told not.

'And the problem is?' Noyes asked, before he raised his glass and drank.

'Miguel Zapata. I don't doubt what he told me, but in a court of law, it's unlikely he'd carry sufficient weight for his evidence to be accepted unquestioned because he's mentally sub-normal. So it's possible, perhaps probable, that at least some of it would be rejected.'

Noyes helped himself to a green olive. He slipped the stone from his mouth to his hand, dropped it into the ashtray. 'Could you trace the purchase of the inflatable?'

'If bought on the island, yes.'

'But if he was thinking smartly, he'll have bought it somewhere else and had it sent over and that could make things very difficult, if not impossible. But if it can be traced, it'll strongly suggest Rook rowed ashore after abandoning his boat ... I suppose the boat's been searched?'

'Yes.'

'And there was no sign of it?'

'No.'

'Assume the purchase can't be traced, so there's only Zapata's evidence, which is dicey. As things stand at the moment, a criminal action to have Rook and his wife charged with attempted fraud would probably fail. But in a civil action to claim the insurance money, which Mrs Rook would initiate, what is required is not proof beyond all reasonable doubt, but proof that Rook is far more likely to be alive than dead. And the evidence we have amassed – my apologies, the evidence you have amassed – will surely do that, even allowing for Miguel's mental incapacity.'

'The insurance company will refuse to pay, leaving the señora to go to court if she's ready to take the risk?'

'That's a decision which will be taken at directors' level, but I'd offer good odds they'll lean that way. And if the wife is sensibly advised, she'll accept the decision and be grateful she and her husband have been smart, or lucky, enough to avoid a criminal charge.'

Alvarez drained his glass. 'Then your visit has been a successful one.'

'Made pleasurable by meeting you.'

He signalled to a passing waiter and called for two more drinks. The waiter asked if they were now ready to order? Alvarez consulted the menu for a second time. Did he have llom amb salsa de nata i xeres or merluza con alcaparras?

Alvarez dialled, leaned back in his chair and rested his feet on the desk.

'Yes?' said the plum-voiced secretary.

'It's Inspector Alvarez from—'

'Wait.'

He used his foot to direct the fan a little to the right. His imagination began to soar. He was on a boat, the island a distant smudge on the horizon. His young, nubile companion said she wanted to go for a swim, but had forgotten a costume. But that really didn't matter, did it, since there was no one to see her skinny—

'Well?' demanded Salas.

'I have to report, señor, on the case of the missing Englishman, Señor Rook.'

'Then report.'

'He did not drown, so he is alive.'

'The usual condition of someone who is not dead.'

'There is sufficient evidence to prove in a civil court that he and his wife have attempted to perpetrate an insurance fraud, so Señor Noyes is returning to England. When we said goodbye, he was kind enough to say my work had been invaluable.'

'In the past, the word signified something without any value.' He cut the connection.

Alvarez removed his feet from the desk, leaned over and opened the bottom right-hand drawer. Never miss the opportunity to celebrate or the chance to celebrate will miss you.

Thirteen

The last day of July. It had been a month of record high temperatures and drought. Farmers who lacked irrigation had only withered crops to show for months of work; however, many of the doctors who treated tourists for sun-inflicted injuries began to plan their holidays at luxury resorts in distant countries.

As he sat behind his desk, Alvarez, for the umpteenth time, used a handkerchief to mop the sweat from his face and neck. He looked at his watch. Still an hour before it would be reasonably safe to return home and begin the weekend, a pleasure marred only by the certainty that Monday must follow Sunday ... He knew a sudden sense of liberation. His delayed holiday began on Monday. He would not have to rise at the crack of dawn; he could stay in bed until he decided it was time to move; he could wander where he wanted or sit in the cool and do nothing. It would be the same on Tuesday, Wednesday, Thursday ... He could perhaps see Gail more often...

The phone awoke him.

'Is that the Cuerpo?'

If the fool at the other end had called the post and asked for him, who the hell did he think he'd be talking to? 'Yes.'

'You've got to come here. A body's in the water, just off the beach.'

'Which beach?'

'Hotel Parelona.'

'Get someone to remove it if it's bothering you.'

'Are you crazy? Of course it's bothering us. The guests can't go swimming.'

'Why not?'

'You are crazy. It's a disgusting idea.'

'Then call the undertakers to remove it.'

'You think we haven't done that. They're here.'

'Then why bother me?'

'They say they can't remove the body until you've examined it.'

'If they've no reason for suspicion—'

'They say it's the rules.'

About to declare that nonsense, he checked his words. He vaguely remembered that recently all members of the Cuerpo had been reminded that in the case of an un-explained death, a thorough investigation of all circumstances was to be made before the body was moved. 'Is it male or female?'

'I don't know.'

'Age?'

'Do you think I've examined it when it's been dead for God knows how long?'

'If you haven't, how do you know it's been dead for a long time?'

'The guest who first saw it when she was swimming says it's in a horrid state. She's having hysterics.'

'Slap her face.'

'Slap a guest's face? You're not just crazy, you're insane. Are you going to come here?'

'I suppose I'll have to. You'd better phone whichever doctor is on police duty.'

'Can't you do that?'

'No.' He replaced the receiver to prevent an argument.

How bitterly true it was that a man had only to congratulate himself all was going well and he'd fall into a cow pat. A Saturday morning when he was about to go off duty and start his holiday and he was faced with a three-quarters of an hour's drive to the hotel – a drive that worried him even to think about – whatever time was necessary to convince others he was doing his job thoroughly, and a three-quarters of an hour's drive back. Not only would he miss pre-lunch drinks, he might even miss lunch. He dialled home.

'What is it?' Dolores demanded.

It sounded as if perhaps something had gone amiss in the kitchen. 'It's Enrique. I'm going to be back late to lunch, so would you be very kind and keep it warm for me?'

There was a pause, then she said: 'This is Saturday. You stop work at an early time on Saturdays.'

'Only when there's nothing urgent...'

'You have something urgent?'

'I have to go to Hotel Parelona.'

There was silence.

'Are you still there?' he asked.

'When do I have the opportunity to be anywhere else?'

'I'm very sorry about this because I know how much you naturally dislike it when someone's not home to enjoy the delicious meal you've taken so much trouble to prepare, but I just can't get back in time.'

'My mother often said to me, "Remember well, daughter, when a man offers you praise, it will come in a poisoned chalice."'

'You reckon I'm lying? Then where d'you think I'm going and why?'

'I cannot put such disgraceful thoughts into words.'

'If they're that shocking, you shouldn't have them.'

'It pleases you to mock me?'

'I'm only trying to make you understand.'

'I am a feeble woman who understands it is my duty to serve uncomplainingly, to suffer in silence the contempt with which my self-sacrifices are treated. Therefore, I will keep your meal warm until you decide you can drag yourself away from your pleasures.'

'Examining a body is hardly—'

'Enough! You shame me!'

'A dead body...' He was talking to a dead line. He replaced the receiver. With typical female stubbornness, she believed he was going to meet Gail. Would that were true. To meet Gail and enjoy her smiles was to find a warm pleasure in life. Why? She did not enjoy great beauty; her direct, quiet manner negated any suggestion of exotic delights. So where lay her attraction? In her calm, warm, friendliness? He sighed. The world was full of mysteries of which the greatest was woman.

The journey over the mountains was one he never began without the conviction he would not complete it. For someone suffering from altophobia, as did he, the drive was a nightmare of tight, unfenced bends, and precipices. By the time he reached the last slope down to the relatively flat land on which the hotel stood, his nerves were so strained that a brandy at the beach bar failed to restore him – but a second would have bankrupted him.

He left the bar and walked along the curving sand, backed by pine trees. In the past, only those who sailed on the occasional ferry from the port and those with cars had had access to the beach, so there had been no crowds and the water had been crystal clear. Then ferries had arrived more frequently and buses brought tourists in their tens of dozens and the beach had become crowded, noisy, litter-strewn, and the water cloudy and polluted. Yet again, tourism destroying that which had attracted it.

When the gentle flow of tourists became a flood, the management of Hotel Parelona had ordered – contrary to the law – that the beach in front of their grounds be fenced off so that its use could be restricted to hotel guests, thereby preserving them from unwanted contact with the hoi polloi. Alvarez pushed his way through the throng of onlookers and ducked under the blue rope cordon, identified himself to a guard. As he walked towards the four men who stood at the water's edge, he stared at what appeared to be a clump of rubbish floating a couple of metres off-shore in the millpond-calm water. It made a mind shiver to understand that that rubbish was a body.

One of the four – all identified as hotel employees by ties and black coats, despite the heat – said: 'Are you the police?'

'Cuerpo.'

'It's taken you long enough to get here.'

Alvarez disliked small, officious men. 'I haven't yet learned to fly.'

'But this is so dreadful for the hotel.'

'I don't suppose it's all that great for the victim.'

'I want the body moved right away.'

'Has the doctor on police duty arrived yet?'

'Not as far as I know.'

'We have to wait until he's here before anything can be done.'

'This is ridiculous.'

'It's the rules.'

'As soon as he arrives, make certain everything is cleared away as quickly as possible.'

'Things will be done according to the book.'

The man, his expression one of angry frustration, walked past Alvarez and across to the steps which led up to the hotel garden.

Mestre, an undertaker from Llueso, said: 'He won't be offering you a free drink.'

'In a hotel like this,' Alvarez said, as he stared at the two top floors which were visible above the bushes growing near the banked edge of the garden, 'only bad advice is free.' He turned. 'I suppose I'd better have a look and see what we have.'

'Damaged goods.'

'Meaning?'

'I'd say he's been dead for well over a month.'

'It's definitely a man?'

'That's about all that's certain, because when a body's been in warm water for a good time—'

'I'd rather not know.'

What at a distance had looked like rubbish

became a body which lay face downwards, arms and legs trailing in the sand; it wore a light blue shirt, linen trousers, and one yachting plimsoll. Alvarez looked across the brilliant blue sea at the mountains on the far side of the bay, briefly seeking beauty as an antidote to the ugliness in front of him.

Dr Vega arrived twenty minutes later. Small, sharply featured, nervously energetic, he had endless time and patience for the ill, but not for the malingerers and the general public. He removed his shoes and socks, rolled up his trousers to above his knees, walked into the water. He briefly examined the body, returned to the beach, told the undertakers to bring it ashore; once it was ashore, he made a second, more thorough examination.

'There's precious little I can tell you,' he said to Alvarez. 'Male, probably early to middle forties. No obvious signs of injury, but in the state of decomposition, that observation is meaningless. Drowning is almost certainly the cause of death which could have taken place some time ago ... You said you hadn't examined the body?'

'I didn't want to disturb anything before you arrived.' He would have learned nothing and the closer one came to death, the sharper one realized there was no escape because life demanded death.

'Have you any idea of his identity?'

'None. As far as I can recall, there are no males in that age bracket reported missing.'

'Then for what it's worth, I'll give you my opinion. He's a wealthy Britisher.'

'What leads you to say that?'

'The watch on his wrist is a gold Patek Philippe. The shirt has the maker's mark, Turnbull and Asser, and I've read that's top English quality. The trousers are probably of equal quality, but no tab is readily visible. There's nothing in any of the pockets.'

'Identifying him is going to be a problem,' Alvarez said despondently.

'There's nothing like a problem to keep a mind active.'

Why was that an advantage?

'I had to keep your meal warm for a very long time,' Dolores said, as she collected Alvarez's plate from the table, 'so it cannot have been as good as I would have wished.'

She had spoken quite pleasantly, suggesting her aggressive mood of the morning had abated. 'It was still absolutely delicious,' he assured her. In truth, the pollasatre en chanfaina had suffered considerably from the delay; one or two portions of chicken had become slightly dried out, the aubergines, green peppers, and tomatoes, overcooked. But one patted a tigress, not pulled its tail.

It seemed she divined his true judgment. 'It would have been better had you managed to arrive home when it was ready.'

'As I would have done if possible, but a man has to do what he is called upon to do.'

'Men have poor hearing.'

'There was a long wait for the doctor. He had to examine the body before it could be moved to the morgue.'

'You had to deal with a dead body?'

'I told you what was happening.'

'You made no mention of that fact.'

'I said over the phone—'

'You said nothing. Where was this?'

'On the beach in front of Hotel Parelona.'

'You have been there all morning?'

'Yes.'

She carried his plate through to the kitchen, returned with four peaches and a plate which she put in front of him. 'Ana promised me these were ready to eat. You'll need a knife.'

'I'll get one.'

'There's no need for you to move after such a busy morning.' She went past him, opened a drawer in the dresser, brought out a knife which she handed to him.

He ate the peach. Conscience – in others – was an admirable emotion. For once, she was behaving like a dutiful woman.

He undressed down to underpants, redirected the fan, lay down on the bed, switched off the overhead light, which had been necessary because the shutters were fast, and closed his eyes. One of the greatest gifts from the gods to man was the siesta – the chance to recover from the morning's toils. He was on the fuzzy path to sleep when a sudden, unwelcome thought jerked him fully awake. He had not reported the finding of the body to Palma. In itself, that was probably not serious. Salas, recently addicted to golf, had probably chosen to be out on a course rather than at the office on a Saturday morning and therefore could hardly complain about slackness. But what was serious was the possibility Salas would order him to delay his holiday yet again until the identity of the dead man was established ... There had to be some way of avoiding this. The obvious one was to discover the deceased's identity. But since there was no report of a missing man in the past weeks, this was going to be far from easy...

Why had no one reported a missing man, probably British? Wealth came in many forms, one of which was drugs. The dead man might have been in drug running and been accidentally lost at sea as a load was being transferred from offshore boat to inshore one. None of his fellow workers would report his death. If that were so, the inquiry would become more complex, yet simpler. Complex because it would be difficult to uncover information, simpler – from his point of view, that was – since all that it would be necessary to do would be to forward what little information there was to the British authorities and leave them to pursue the case. Further, Salas would not raise any objection to pursuing this course because it would relieve the Cuerpo of any further involvement. He smiled as he relaxed and fell asleep, once more a happy man.

He awoke and was not a happy man. Whilst he'd slept, his subconscious had been active and provided an alternative to the identity of the dead man – a solution which should have occurred to him long ago.

Fourteen

There was no parking space in Carrer Por-
reres or in Carrer Juan Trilla. Alvarez swore.
Soon there would be no parking space on
the island. Then a car pulled out ahead of
him and he hurriedly turned into the gap.
He raised the window to leave a couple of
centimetres gap at the top – it was self-
deception to believe that would ensure the
interior of the car did not become an oven
within a quarter of an hour – stepped out on
to the pavement, locked the car and began to
walk. After only a few paces, he was sweating
heavily, breathing quickly, and reluctantly
remembering his doctor's advice that if he
wished to draw his pension, he should give
up smoking and greatly reduce his eating
and drinking.

He reached 31 Carrer Porreros, opened
the front door and stepped into the entrada,
called out. A middle-aged woman came
through the inner doorway.

Aguenda was known for her abrupt, often
rudely so, manner. There were those who
said Jiminez looked forward to the time

when she became one of his clients. 'Is Eduardo here?'

'And if he is?'

'I'd like a word with him.'

She went back through the doorway.

The entrada was typically, yet untypically, furnished. The chest was covered with a linen cloth embroidered with a Mallorquin pattern of blue flowers, but the embroidery had been done with professional, not home, skill. The four chairs against the white-washed walls were of luxurious quality, not locally made with leather backing and rush seats. Leafy house plants – usually uninspiring aspidistras – had been replaced by three bonsai almond trees, perfect miniatures. Jiminez was clearly a wealthy man, but then he had one of the few jobs in which continuity of employment was guaranteed.

Jiminez, dressed in vest and trousers, worn slippers on his feet, entered. 'Not a business call, I hope?'

'My business, not yours.'

'And no one's told you it's a Sunday?' Jiminez laughed. 'Come on through.'

They went into a sitting room, over-furnished and suffering a very large flat-screen television. 'I'll tell her to make coffee,' Jiminez said.

A moment later, Alvarez could just hear Aguenda asking if she did not have enough to do without making coffee for everyone who called at the house. Women seemed forever to complain about overwork.

Jiminez returned with two glasses well filled with brandy; he handed one to Alvarez, sat. 'What's so serious it brings the inspector here on a Sunday? Has someone shot the superior chief?'

'Would that was the reason.' The brandy, whilst not of top quality, was of a better one than they drank at home. Hors d'Age? 'You pulled a body out of the sea yesterday...'

'Which was a job and a half because of the state it was in.'

Alvarez tried not to listen to the detailed description, but inevitably some of the words registered. How did the prayer run which was used for burial at sea? Commit the body to the deep, to be turned into corruption. How true. When Jiminez finished speaking, he said: 'Dr Vega said the dead man was wearing a gold watch...'

'And you think it isn't in the safe, waiting to be claimed by a relative?' Jiminez demanded with sudden, sharp anger.

'Of course not.'

'Since I was a lad, there's not been so much as a button gone missing.'

'I know I can safely die with my pockets stuffed full of euro notes and they'll rot with me.'

'Get buried like that and your superiors will be asking questions!' Jiminez laughed, his good humour restored. 'All right, then, if you don't reckon I've helped myself, what's your interest in the watch?'

'I'm wondering if it could offer proof of identity?'

'There is something engraved on the back of it.'

'What?'

'Can't say. Just noticed there were some marks when I dropped the watch into the envelope to put into the safe.'

'Then I'd like to have a look at it.'

'Easily done. But there's no rush before Aguenda's made the coffee and we've maybe had another little coñac.'

It was twenty-five minutes before Jiminez led the way into a room at the back of the house which was used as an office. He crossed to a free-standing safe. 'I keep things here and not at work so as I know no one else is taking an interest. D'you remember when you didn't have to worry about such things? When you could leave the house unlocked and not lose so much as a spoon? Things have changed.'

'It's called progress.'

Jiminez went over to the small desk, pulled open the right-hand top drawer, brought out two keys; he unlocked the safe and produced a large brown envelope.

'If I were you,' Alvarez said, 'I'd find somewhere else to keep the keys.'

'Why's that?'

'If someone breaks in to steal what's going, the first place he'll look for the keys will be the desk.'

'You reckon?'

'I know.'

'It's easier if they're handy. Still, if you say.' He held out the envelope.

As Alvarez took it, he wondered if Jiminez would move the keys to a safer place. Probably not. Mallorquins regarded with suspicion advice for which they had not paid. What was the advisor hoping to gain? On the envelope was written 'Client unknown' and the date. He opened it, slid out the gold wristwatch and strap on to the palm of his hand. A thing of beauty? That depended on how much it had cost. He turned it over and on the back two letters had been so elaborately engraved it took him a moment to be certain they were M and G. He dropped the watch back into the envelope, handed that to Jiminez.

'Do you now know who the dead man is?'

'I think so, but I'll have to talk to someone before I can be certain.' Why was it that one's best wishes seldom came true, but one's worst fears often did?

Alvarez climbed the steps and rang the bell. Diego opened the door. 'Is the señora here?'

'She's down by the pool as far as I know.

What brings you back now?'

'I need to have a word with her.'

'Enjoy it.'

'Why's that?'

'She's in a foul mood.'

'For any particular reason?'

'How would I know? Her kind create trouble when they've nothing better to do.'

Alvarez stepped into the hall.

'You must know the way by now, so you can see yourself down to the pool.'

Lazy bastard, Alvarez thought. He went into the sitting room, delightfully cool since the air-conditioning was on, and through to the garden. As he made his way down the slightly sloping lawn, he saw Gloria look up and then adjust the top of her bikini. A pity.

Her greeting was short. 'Why the hell are you back here?'

'To ask you something, señora.'

'Didn't you ask enough questions before?'

It became even more difficult to brace himself to give bad news when her manner was so confrontational. 'It is very important.'

'Then hurry it up.'

'Did ... Does the señor own a wristwatch?'

'Good God, of course he does! D'you think we live in the Stone Age?'

'What make is it?

'What does that matter to you?'

'Please, señora, tell me what make is his watch.'

'A Patek Philippe.'

'Is there an inscription on it?' He wished he could remove her dark glasses and note the expression in her eyes.

'Why are you asking?' Her tone was now uncertain, not aggressive.

'I will explain as soon as you have answered me.'

'I had our initials engraved on the back.'

'What letters would they be?'

'G and M. What on earth do you think they'd be?'

'Señora, I am deeply sorry to have to tell you that a gold Patek Philippe wristwatch with those initials engraved on the back was worn by a man whose body was washed up on the beach yesterday morning.'

She stared at him for several seconds before she shouted: 'You're lying!'

'No señora, I am not.'

'It can't be.'

'I have seen the watch.'

'It's not his.'

'I will have to ask you to examine the watch to confirm that.'

'I won't.'

He hesitated, then said: 'I will return at another time and bring the watch here.'

'Why won't you understand? It can't be Maurice.'

Her panic was evident; but her question inevitably raised another. 'But the señor

162

sadly is missing.'

She looked away.

Her emotional reaction, he thought as he slowly walked up towards the house, had been typical of someone who had been given unexpected bad news. But then Noyes had named her a passable actress.

As Alvarez entered the post, the duty cabo at the desk said: 'You're so dedicated to your work, you turn up here today? Or had you forgotten you're on holiday?'

Alvarez continued in dignified silence, climbed the stairs, briefly halted at the top to regain his breath, continued to his room and slumped down in the chair behind the desk. It wasn't dedication which had brought him, it was self-preservation. Salas had to hear what had happened from him, not another source, or he would be accused of gross incompetence.

He lit a cigarette before he remembered he had promised himself to smoke far less; he considered stubbing it out, but waste was indefensible. He lifted the receiver and dialled.

'Yes?' said the plum-voiced secretary.

'It's Inspector Alvarez speaking and I—'

'Wait.'

'What do you want?' Salas finally demanded.

'I have to report—'

'I understood you were starting your holiday today.'

'That is so, señor, but I decided I had to come in to work.'

'Are you ill?'

'No, señor.'

'Then is this your unfortunate idea of humour?'

'I have to report that the body of a drowned man has been washed up on Parelona beach and there is reason to believe he is Maurice Rook.'

There was a silence which Salas finally broke. 'Fool!'

'I assure you that is correct—'

'Fool that I was not to have understood that when you assured me beyond question he was alive, this was virtually a guarantee he was dead.'

'But I'm wondering if he really is.'

'Is what?'

'Dead.'

'Have you not just told me his body has been washed up on the beach?'

'Yes, señor.'

'Yet now you wonder if he's really dead. If you are not ill—'

'I don't think you understand what I'm trying to say.'

'The Delphic oracle was a model of lucidity compared to you.'

'The drowned man is certainly dead.'

'You're quite certain that is established in your mind?'

'And there is evidence to point to the fact the dead man is Maurice Rook, but I still think it possible he is alive.'

'Then I suggest you consult a psychiatrist at the earliest opportunity.'

'Señor, if you were planning an insurance scam—'

'You will not suggest such an absurd impossibility.'

'If I were planning an insurance scam on a very big scale, I would know my disappearance must be treated with considerable suspicion and the insurance company would not pay up until a thorough investigation had been carried out; even then, it might withhold payment, forcing me to go to court to suffer all the uncertainties one meets in law. The one way of avoiding all that is to produce a body that is identified as me.

'I have not the slightest doubt that Señor Rook, with the help of his wife, planned an insurance fraud. He may have hoped – criminals often suffer blind optimism – that his disappearance would be accepted without question as being proof of death, but was sufficiently smart to accept that might not be so. Therefore, faced with the urgent need of money, he decided he must provide a corpse which would be accepted as his.'

'What is the identifying evidence?'

'A gold wristwatch on the back of which are the initials G and M. I have spoken to Señora Rook and she says those initials were inscribed on the back of her husband's watch. Since the odds against a Patek Philippe watch with those initials belonging to someone else are very considerable, it would seem to offer definite identification. Of course, she will have to see the watch and confirm it is his.'

'How did she react to the possibility her husband is dead?'

'With a shocked refusal to believe it.'

'Were her emotions genuine?'

'They seemed so, but as Señor Noyes once remarked, she is an actress.'

'Is there anything more to report?'

'Only that I suggest Señor Noyes is asked if he can provide us with means of identification which will prove the dead man cannot be Señor Rook.'

'An efficient officer would have already done so,' said Salas, before he cut the connexion.

Fifteen

'Sorry to have kept you waiting,' Noyes said over the telephone, 'but I was in a meeting and the secretary didn't have the sense to say it was urgent. What's the news? You're coming over here for your holidays so that I can have the pleasure of introducing you to the culinary pleasures of boiled cabbage and spotted dick?'

'Regretfully, I must stay here and work because a body has been washed on to Parelona beach and it was wearing a watch which provisionally has been identified as Señor Rook's.'

'Good God!'

'There is the problem that the body has been in the water for some weeks and decomposition has made any visual identification virtually impossible.'

'And you have your doubts?'

'If I were trying to defraud an insurance company of a million pounds, I would know my disappearance was unlikely to be sufficient proof of my death for many months, perhaps years, but my need for money cannot allow a long wait. Therefore it becomes necessary to provide a corpse which will be accepted as mine. A watch which can be shown to have belonged to me does provide identification, but when a million pounds is at stake, will that be sufficient? This means, it must not be obvious that the body is not mine. As you will know, probably better than I, fire is often used for that purpose. A body is found in a burned-out car belonging to an individual who is missing and on the body is something which has survived the fire and can be identified as his. In this case, decomposition has been used instead of fire. Rook found a man of his age and build whose disappearance would hardly be noted – not difficult since there are many drop-outs, beachcombers, men who lead little more than a vagrant's life, on the island. He drugged or plied his victim with alcohol until he was incapable and then drowned him.'

'How could Rook be certain decomposition would reach the stage where visual identification was impossible before the body was washed ashore?'

'By planning well ahead.'

'He killed the man and kept the body immersed until satisfied it was in a suitable condition? That's pretty macabre.'

'A million pounds changes a man's susceptibilities.'

'I guess you want me to find if it's possible to determine some physical characteristic of Rook's which will disprove the corpse is his. It could be difficult since it's a little time since he moved out of England, but I'll do what I can. Teeth are often a good platform for comparison. Let's hope his dentist has kept records. Failing anything else, either you or I can ask for photographic identification. Comparisons made by measuring physical ratios may not be sufficient to confirm identification, but it is accepted as good evidence to deny it.'

Ten minutes later, Alvarez replaced the receiver and settled back in the chair. Despite the wristwatch, he was certain the body was not that of Rook. A greater man than Salas would have praised him for his acuity in not accepting the obvious, but the superior chief was small both in stature and character.

Marta opened the front door of Son Raldo. 'Not you back after all this time!'

Alvarez stepped inside. 'Maybe you can tell me how...' He stopped as Gail came through the far doorway. Her greeting was friendly. Her short shorts disturbed him.

'I suppose you want to see Gloria?' she asked.

'I should like to, yes.'

'I think I'll have a word with her and make

certain she's up to it; if she isn't, you'll have to return another time to speak to her. But come on through.'

As he followed her, he noticed how snugly her shorts fitted, what little depth of material guarded her modesty ... He cursed his mind which insisted on concentrating on irrelevant matters.

She came to a stop in the middle of the sitting room. 'Isn't it merienda time?'

'I suppose it is,' he answered, ignoring the fact he had had his merienda before leaving Llueso.

'I'll ask Marta to make some coffee. I won't be a moment.'

He watched her leave, then sat and tried to occupy his mind with thoughts of high moral value.

She returned. 'Gloria's sorry, but she really can't face any more questions.'

'She is very distressed?'

'I'm afraid so.'

Or playing the part of a woman who had learned her missing husband was dead, knowing it was some vagrant's body which had worn his expensive watch? 'I wonder if you'd help me, then?'

'If I can, of course I will.'

'Do you know if Señor Rook ever visited a doctor or a dentist here, on the island?'

'Why on earth do you want to know that?'

'Sadly, it is necessary to confirm the body

170

is that of the señor because...'

'Well?'

How could he explain without shocking her? 'It was ... well, rather a long time ago when the señor fell into the water...'

'I think I understand,' she said, in a low voice.

'I know this must be as painful for you as for the señora, even if, as you mentioned, your relationship with your uncle was not very close. I am so sorry to have to cause you such distress.'

'You really mean that, don't you?' She looked out at the garden as she spoke. 'I wonder if you can begin to understand how it helps to meet someone who's genuinely sympathetic? It makes everything ... just about bearable.'

Marta entered, a tray in her hands. She held it for Gail to help herself to sugar and milk, did the same for Alvarez, saying that the brandy was for him.

'You were asking if Maurice visited a doctor or a dentist?' Gail said, as Marta closed the door behind herself. 'As far as I know, he didn't visit a doctor; he never seemed to suffer from as much as a cold. But they both had a check-up at the dentist every six months, or so.'

'Do you know which dentist?'

'In Playa Neuva. She's very efficient. Her name is...' She thought, stirring her coffee as she did so. Then, as she withdrew the spoon, she said: 'Juana Pons. She comes from some-where in South America. Chile, possibly.'

'Thank you.'

'Is there anything more I can tell you?'

'I don't think so.'

'Then can we talk about something else? Tell me some more about the history of the island. It's so lovely, where we foreigners aren't responsible for ruining it, that it must have been the home of at least one of the gods of ancient times.'

He would never have called himself a good raconteur, but her rapt attention suggested he was a better one than he acknowledged.

It was almost lunchtime when he said: 'I must go.' He stood. 'I wonder if...' He be-came silent.

'Am I allowed to know what you're won-dering?'

'Would you have dinner with me one even-ing?'

She smiled. 'With pleasure.'

When he left the house to cross to his car, he felt as if he were walking a few inches above the ground.

The lift started with a shudder that made him fear it was going to lunge down to destruction or stop and imprison him for hours, then it rose smoothly to the second floor. A white-coated assistant behind a small, semicircular counter asked if he had an appointment. He thankfully explained he had not come for treatment, identified himself, and said he would like a word with Señora Pons. He was asked to wait in the room to the left.

The only other occupant was a middle-aged woman who looked as apprehensive as he would have done had he been awaiting treatment. As he sat and picked up a two-month-old copy of *¡Hola!*, he thought he heard the shrill scream of a drill; he winced.

Fifteen minutes later, after a man had left, an assistant called him into a room filled with all the usual instruments of torture. Juana Pons was middle-aged and attractive, but authoritative – if she said a tooth should come out, out it came.

'So what brings you here, Inspector?' she asked in a deep, tuneful voice.

'To ask you if you had Señor Rook as a patient.'

'Why do you want to know?'

'You have not perhaps heard he disappeared while at sea on his boat?'

'I have not, no. I'm sorry to hear that,' she said formally.

'Recently a body has been recovered and I am having to make certain enquiries concerning it. It will greatly help me if you can provide a chart of Señor Rook's teeth.'

'The dead man may be he?'

'It is possible.'

'I'll get Cristina to look up his records and provide you with a copy of the chart.'

He thanked her and returned to the waiting room, grateful to do so without having suffered dental assault. Moments later, Cristina handed him an envelope inside which was a sheet of thick paper on which were printed representations of an upper and lower jaw; against some of the teeth, notes had been made. To him they were meaningless, to an expert, they would prove the dead man was not Rook.

Alvarez was trying to decide whether, since he was meant to be on holiday, he was on general or only specific duty. Was he concerned that one of the supermarkets had reported a team of pickpockets, almost certainly from eastern Europe, were operating in the store and already three clients had complained of losses, or could he ignore the complaint? After all, most of the clients would be foreigners and the supermarket's problem had nothing to do with Rook ... There was a phone call.

'Morning, Enrique. What's the weather like?' Noyes asked.

'So hot, it is dangerous to do anything more than sit in the shade and enjoy a cool drink.'

'If you say anything more, I'll be out on the

next plane ... We've managed to contact a doctor who dealt with Rook before he left here. Some years ago, he fell and broke his right leg severely. No contemporary records or X-rays have been kept, but the doctor has given a description of the fracture which, according to him, will identify the old injury to a fair degree of certainty. I'll send you his report by fax as soon as we sign off.'

'Then I think we have all we need since I have a copy of Señor Rook's dental chart.'

'When will the PM be?'

'Soon. But I can't say more than that for the moment.'

'You'll let me know the result, won't you?'

'I can give it to you now.'

Noyes chuckled.

'Are the directors of the insurance company interested in results?'

'What do you expect when the size of their annual bonuses depends on whether or not the company has to pay out a million on a doubtful claim?'

If only he knew what an annual bonus was.

The post-mortem result reached him on Monday. He opened the envelope and put the typewritten sheets of paper down on the desk, but did not immediately read them. Salas would have to commend him. He had had the imagination to believe an insurance fraud had been intended; to foresee the course Rook would have taken to perpetrate that fraud; to look beyond the obvious...

He opened the bottom right-hand drawer of the desk and brought out bottle and glass. A man who had proved himself deserved a drink.

He read the report. The dental charts and an X-ray, together with the information from England, confirmed beyond fear of contradiction that the body was that of Maurice Rook...

The bloody fools had forgotten to add 'not'; or in his excitement, he was reading what was not written ... He read the first paragraph four times. The dead man remained Maurice Rook. He poured himself a second drink, convinced that a third would be needed before he began to overcome the sense of resentful shock. Eventually he read the rest of the report. Prior to death, Rook had suffered a blow to the front of his head, an injury not immediately obvious because of decomposition. This blow probably caused considerable mental confusion rather than unconsciousness. The blow could not have been self-inflicted, could have been delivered by a third party, or have been received in a fall. The object which caused the injury was solid, probably metal or wood, round, about two centimetres in diameter.

It seemed Rook might have tripped and hit

his head on something, become semi-conscious, and fallen overboard. Accident. Or someone had delivered a blow. Murder. He poured himself the third drink, knowing this would not deliver him from the trouble to come. But as the ancients used to say, sell your cow tomorrow if you do not have to do so today.

He stood on the quayside and wondered if he really did have to board *Corrina* again. But Salas was bound to ask if he had examined the boat to note if there was any indication of where Rook had fallen or what was the object which had been used to kill him. If he could answer in the affirmative, Salas would have one less scourge with which verbally to beat him.

He slowly climbed the gangplank, fighting the perverse desire to look down and suffer the mental panic of doing so, stepped on to the afterdeck, sweating, breathless, his heart racing. He unlocked the saloon, remembered the small bar at the for'd end, hurriedly made his way there. There were three shelves, with individual fiddles to hold the bottles firm in a rough sea, and he chose a half-full Courvoisier VSOP. When he drained the glass, he felt partially restored.

He searched the accommodation, wheelhouse and decks (to make certain, inter alia, that as he had previously claimed, there was no small inflatable aboard). He found no marks to suggest where someone had fallen nor anything round and hard, a couple of centimetres in diameter, which could have been used as a weapon. He walked aft, satisfied he could now truthfully claim to have searched every centimetre of the the boat without success.

What one climbed, one had to descend and from where he stood at the head of the gangplank, it was all too obvious there was a chasm between boat and quay. He began to sweat, though not from the heat, his lungs were squeezed, his heart thumped. There was only one thing to do. He returned to the saloon and poured himself another cognac.

Once more aft, he girded his mental loins. But about to step on to the gangplank, he realized that since there was a gap in the rails – to make it very much easier to board or go ashore – there must, in the name of safety, be a way of plugging that gap when at sea. Sockets on the stanchions on either side of the gap identified the necessary object as almost certainly a length of rail with a lug at each end which slotted into the sockets. He had seen no such object anywhere on the boat.

He used the first two joints of his forefinger to gauge the diameter of the rails. About two centimetres. Not proof that the missing length had been used as a weapon and then thrown overboard, but an indication. Yet if that was a potential weapon, then all the top rails were potential causes of Rook's injury. He examined the rails along each side of the boat and found no traces of contact – no imprints, no adhering hairs, no dried blood.

He was so pleased at his astuteness in identifying the probable missing weapon that he was halfway down the gangplank before he began to suffer the fear, and the lure, of falling into the abyss.

He drove – too hot to walk – the short distance to the boatyard and spoke to Fiol, who, bad temperedly, called his foreman up to the office. The foreman could give Alvarez no information concerning the missing rail.

Sixteen

Alvarez sat at his desk, switched on the fan, looked at the phone, slumped back in the chair. It had turned into one of those afternoons one longed to forget. He'd had trouble falling asleep after lunch – a portent of medical problems? – and when he'd finally succeeded in doing so, he had suffered a nightmare in which he had become lost in an unknown city and a man – never seen, but undoubtedly Salas – had stalked him, threatening to kill him by telephone. Dolores had been in one of her peculiar moods and had not bought fresh coca for him to have with his chocolate. Troubles hunted in packs. Now, he had to make that phone call...

He picked up the receiver, dialled, said he wanted to speak to the superior chief. He was told to wait. He stared at the shuttered window and wondered if it would be possible to apply for early retirement on the grounds of stress. Then he could spend his declining days growing tomatoes, beans, peas, onions, carrots ... Some of the tomatoes could be stuffed with that magical mixture Dolores's mother had taught her to make – odd, that, since the mixture was sweet, not bitter...

'Yes?'

'It's Inspector Alvarez, señor—'

'You imagine I have not been informed of that unfortunate fact? What do you want?'

'I have received the post-mortem report on the man whose body was washed up at Cap Parelona. It is estimated he had been dead for some weeks, but no accurate figure can be given because of the length of immersion and the high temperatures of the water. It is confirmed he died from drowning. However, prior to his death, he suffered a blow to the head which was not apparent before the post-mortem because of the state of decomposition. The blow could not have been self-inflicted and might have occurred when he fell—'

'No doubt because he was tight.'

'His blood/alcohol level was not high. There is another possibility, that the injury to his head was inflicted. Someone hit him with a solid object.'

'How very typical! A man is washed ashore in what starts as a simple case of accidental drowning, but after you have begun to investigate the case, there is the possibility of murder.'

'Señor, the facts—'

'Facts are precise, unambiguous, and

181

comprehensible. You are a stranger to facts.'

'I boarded *Corrina*—'

'Where are we wandering to now?'

'*Corrina* is his boat, on which he sailed...'

'You feel the need to acquaint me with details of which I am fully aware?'

'The circumstances are somewhat complicated...'

'They will be by now.'

'As I said earlier—'

'Then there is no need to repeat yourself.'

'I boarded *Corrina* to determine whether there was evidence of a fall – which there was not – or there was something which could have provided a weapon of approximately two centimetres in diameter—'

'Would it trouble you too much to explain why you were searching for a weapon of that size?'

'I was just about to—'

'Your ability to be about to do something is infinite; your ability actually to do it, infinitesimal.'

'The PM report said the wound was caused, either accidentally or deliberately, by something solid, round, and approximately two centimetres in diameter. The rails of the boat are of such size and I noticed there was obviously a length at the back of the boat which was removable to allow one to board; there was no sign of this. Yet at sea, it must be in place for safety. It could be this was used to strike the deceased, then was thrown overboard to make certain it could never offer any evidence.'

'The deceased was knocked on the head, he fell or was pushed overboard, and drowned?'

'If he didn't accidentally fall against the rails—'

'How do you intend to determine what happened?'

'I will first find out if anyone had a motive for wishing him dead because if there is someone, it may well be murder; if there is not, it becomes more likely he died from an accidental fall.'

'You have just said it was not.'

'Not what, señor?'

'Talking to you is like conversing with a cryptic crossword puzzle. You have said it seemed unlikely he died from an accidental fall.'

'No, señor. I said I could find nothing on which there was evidence to suggest he might have fallen on to it and suffered such an injury. But lack of evidence does not, as you will know, necessarily mean something did not happen. It's the difference between negative and positive.'

'You recognize there is a difference?'

'One fact which obviously has to be taken into account is that at sea a boat may roll even in what appears to be a calm sea because of a slight swell, making it all too easy to lose one's balance and fall. The act of falling makes ordinary judgments regarding the direction of a blow unreliable because the body may be at an angle and momentum may cause—'

'I have suffered sufficient confusion for the day. You will determine whether it was murder or accidental death and will keep me informed at all times; let me repeat that – at all times.' The line went dead.

Alvarez replaced the receiver. Salas had not asked him the identity of the dead man. Perhaps he had been born under a lucky star after all.

The phone rang. He lifted the receiver. 'Inspector Alvarez, Cuerpo General—'

'Have you never learned to deliver a responsible report?' Salas demanded.

'Yes, señor.'

'No, you have not, since you omitted to tell me the most important fact. Have you yet determined the identity of the dead man and if not, why not?'

His mind raced as he tried to find a way of avoiding the unavoidable.

'Well?'

'There was some doubt...'

'Since you are conducting the investigation, that is to be expected.'

'The circumstances were confusing...'

'His name?'

'It eventually became clear that ... in fact, he was Maurice Rook.'

'I'm asking who the dead man is, not the perpetrator of the attempted insurance fraud.'

'Maurice Rook, señor.'

There was a long silence.

'It is virtually impossible to have a logical conversation with you, so perhaps I should not be as astounded as I am that you are incapable of understanding a simple question. However, I will, being a man of consummate patience, try once more. What is the identity of the dead man who was washed ashore at Cap Parelona?'

'Maurice Rook.'

There was another long pause, then: 'Are you trying to tell me that the dead man is Rook?'

'Yes, señor.'

'The man whom you assured me was alive and well, despite his apparent disappearance at sea?'

'It's because—'

'And did you not assure me only days ago that although you did not know who the dead man was, you could be absolutely certain he was not Rook?'

'It seemed—'

'Yet now you assure me with equal certainty that he is Rook. Should I prepare myself for the next transmogrification of this man who flits between life and death with the agility of a dragonfly?' Salas slammed down the receiver.

Alvarez sighed as he reached down to the bottom right-hand drawer of the desk.

Seventeen

Gail's tone was sharp. 'It's not fair to upset her again after all this time.'

'I know,' Alvarez said sadly.

'It had to be a tragic accident.'

'Unfortunately, there is the possibility it was not, which is why I have to question the señora.'

'How can you believe she will be able to tell you anything?'

'She may know if there was someone who had reason to dislike the señor.'

'Are you now suggesting one of his friends murdered him?'

'I am just trying to determine the truth.'

She turned round, took two paces towards the French windows in the sitting room, stopped, turned back. 'I'm sorry, Enrique.'

'For what?'

'Going for you when you're only doing your job. But Gloria is emotionally shattered and I'm trying to do what I can to help her. I know that if you ask her more questions, it will make things even worse.'

'I'll be as brief as possible.'

187

'But as kind as you are...' She stopped, hesitated, then continued. 'Wait here and I'll have a word with Gloria. I'll try to explain why it's so important she sees you and judge how she reacts.'

He watched her leave. Most women who wore shorts could never have seen themselves in a mirror; she could face her image and be proud.

The air-conditioning unit began one of its cycles and he felt a swirl of cold air. Wealth insulated one from much of the world ... Yet it had not insulated Rook from death.

Gloria entered, crossed to a chair, sat. 'Gail says you have to talk to me,' she said dully.

She was dressed in a simple cotton frock, wore no make-up; her hair had been combed, but not groomed. Strange, he thought, how lack of concern for her appearance made her more warmly attractive; ironic that tragedy was responsible for the improvement. 'I am very sorry to have to bother you at so sad a time, señora.'

She continued to stare at the carpet in front of her.

He had known contempt for both her and her husband – wealthy people who had lacked the courage to work honestly to restore their fortunes; now, he experienced a measure of sympathy for her despite the possibility her grief was false. 'Señora, unfortunately some of my questions may be disturbing, but they have to be asked.'

She looked briefly at him, then back at the carpet.

'There is reason to think...' How did one put it into words which would not hurt too much? He spoke quickly. 'Did the señor have enemies?'

'Enemies?'

'Was there someone who had reason, or believed there was reason, to hate your husband?'

She began to fidget her fingers together. 'Why d'you ask?'

'Before he fell into the sea, your husband suffered a blow to the head which probably made him incapable of keeping his balance and he fell overboard. The blow could have been caused by his tripping and hitting something, but I could find no traces to suggest this happened; alternatively, he could have been struck by a solid, round object. There is a removable length of rail at the back of the boat and this is missing.'

'What are you saying? That ... that someone...'

'I have to determine whether his death was accidental or deliberate.'

She stared at him for several seconds, her expression fixed, then began to sob; her body shook as tears slid down her cheeks. He had seldom felt so useless. She stood suddenly, rushed out of the room.

Gail entered. 'Did you have to do that?'

'I had to question her.'

'But there can't have been any need...' She came to a sudden stop. 'Oh, God! Here I go again, shouting at you when it's not your fault. One of my teachers used to say my tongue was always ahead of my brain. Look, Gloria isn't capable now of telling you anything more and heaven only knows when she'll calm down, so is there any way in which I can help?'

'I'm not certain.'

'Then why not find out? And suppose we stay here in the cool since it's burning hot outside, even in the shade of the patio.' She sat. 'What is it you need to know?'

'Has the señor recently had a bitter row with anyone?'

'You think someone he knew killed him?'

'It's not that straightforward. The evidence is thin and ambiguous. The señor might have fallen and suffered a head injury or he might have been hit. It is very unlikely he would have been attacked for no reason, which means that if I identify someone with a motive, the possibility of assault becomes stronger; if there is no such person, it is likely he tripped and fell, hit his head on some part of the boat despite the fact I can find no likely point of contact and the rail is missing.'

'What rail?'

'At the back of the boat...'

'The stern ... Sorry, but Maurice was the archetypal amateur yachtsman – cap, blazer, and every part of the boat to be named in sea language – unfortunately, that sort of thing is catching. You were saying that at the stern, the rail is missing?'

'The section which can be removed.'

'Why is its absence important?'

'If the señor was assaulted, the length of rail might have been the weapon used. And an assailant would have thrown it over the side in order to make certain it could never be found and used to inculpate him.'

'I understand that, but it might be missing simply because Maurice never retrieved it.'

'In what way?'

'You know it has a lug at each end to secure it to the stanchions?'

'I guessed as much.'

'One of the lugs became bent and the rail could be removed or slotted into place only after considerable effort and in Maurice's case, much swearing. He became so annoyed that he decided to get the lug straightened. Perhaps the work hadn't been done before he sailed off to Mahon.'

'Where would he have taken it?'

'The boatyard, probably.'

'They have not had it in for repair.'

'Then he'll have taken it somewhere else. He often complained about the prices the boatyard charged, so he'll have decided to save some euros ... You really think someone used that as a weapon?'

'It has to be a possibility.'

'God! It's become a nightmare ... But I'm sure you'll find someone has mended the rail and it just hasn't been collected.'

'Until that happens, I have to consider the possibility it was not an accident. So I must ask you again, did the señor have a bitter row with someone recently?'

'When does a row become bitter? He had an argument with one person which became slightly heated, but that can't be of any consequence.'

'Why not?'

'I can't imagine Derek Carr killing anything larger than a wasp. He hasn't an inch of backbone in him or he wouldn't let Vivien boss him around as she does.'

Did women become bossy from a sense of insecurity or of inferiority? 'Nevertheless, perhaps I should have a word with him. Will you tell me where he lives?'

After a pause, she did so.

'How did Señor Rook get on with other people?'

'He was always very friendly; some were equally friendly in return.'

'Only some?'

'In the main, the British resent success.'

'There would have been people who hated

him just because of his wealth?'

'Hate is too strong a word. They disliked him from a sense of jealousy. Which, naturally, didn't stop their accepting his invitations and drinking as much champagne as they could swallow.'

'I understand that when the señora was away, the señor entertained other ladies?'

'As someone wrote, to be interesting, a rumour has to be libellous or absurd.'

'He did not entertain other women?'

'In the sense in which you're hinting at? I'm sorry, but his private life is nothing to do with you.'

'A cuckolded husband can be very angry.'

'And now you're suggesting ... Doubting Thomas wouldn't get a look-in when you're around.' A few seconds later, she said: 'Shit! There I go again! And if someone did kill Maurice, I want the man to be made to suffer. But I just can't accept this disintegration of Maurice as I always knew him ... I'm horribly confused, Enrique.'

'Then I will not increase your confusion.'

'No more questions, insinuations, or accusations?'

'None.'

'It may not sound like it, but I really do know that if it were left just to you, you'd try never to upset anyone.'

He stood. 'I must still speak with the señora, but I will do so at another time. One can only hope that then it will be a little less painful for her.'

'I doubt that it can be. But perhaps she'll have found a greater self-control ... Will you do something for me?'

'If I can.'

'Don't try to find out from her if she knew Maurice was having an affair.'

'Then he was?'

'Please, Enrique.'

'Sorry. When I speak to her, I will suggest nothing.'

'Thank you.'

He saw gratitude in her deep brown eyes; he hoped she did not see hypocrisy in his. He would honour his promise, but Gloria must judge from his questions, his reason for asking them.

He parked, walked the hundred metres along the pavement, went into the entrada, as spotlessly clean as ever, and through to the sitting/dining room.

Dolores stepped through the bead curtain. 'I don't have to ask why you're late again,' she said sharply.

'Late?' He indicated the table. 'It's not laid yet.'

'It would not occur to you I have not had time to do that because I have been slaving in the kitchen; or that I was hoping you might return in time to offer to save me the

194

trouble. Of course, I have always been absurdly optimistic where men are concerned ... You can lay the table now.'

Tasks shared were tasks halved. 'Where's Jaime?'

'You expect me to know where my husband hides himself from work?'

'And the children?'

'Having lunch with Luisa. If you have finished arguing, I will return to the kitchen and continue slaving.' She swept through the bead curtain.

He sat at the table. Despite Dolores's female humour, it was clear lunch was not imminent. He reached across and opened the sideboard, brought out a bottle of Soberano and a glass, poured himself a drink. He would have welcomed ice, but that necessitated going into the kitchen.

The front door was slammed shut and a moment later, Jaime entered the room. He looked at the table. 'No glass for me? Look after yourself, won't you, and to hell with anyone else.'

'She wants you to lay the table before you have a drink.'

'Why?'

'Perhaps so that we can eat.'

'Why isn't she going to do it?'

'Ask her.'

Jaime crossed to the sideboard and brought out a glass. He sat, picked up the bottle, poured himself a drink. 'In the old days, a woman didn't try to tell a man what to do.'

Dolores said, as she came through the bead curtain: 'Because she knew he became deaf the moment he was asked to lift a finger.' She stared at the table. 'And it is easy to see nothing has changed.'

'When a man's been working bloody hard...' Jaime began.

'A circumstance about which you are not qualified to speak.' She turned to Alvarez. 'Your morning has been spent agreeably?'

'Very far from it.'

'You have not enjoyed being with your foreign woman?'

'As a matter of fact—'

'Why does a man so often preface his lies with those words?'

'I had to question the English woman whose husband disappeared and since has been found dead.'

'And your friend was not there?'

'As a matter of fact...' He stopped.

'Ha!' she said scornfully.

'My relationship with her is purely a professional one.'

'I imagine that description could not be more apt,' she snapped, before she returned into the kitchen.

Eighteen

From downstairs came another call. 'You must hurry because it's late.'

'Late' was a word difficult to define. Alvarez raised his arm to look at his watch and was surprised to discover it was almost five o'clock. By any definition he could think of, he was going to be late back to the post. He swivelled round on the bed until he was sitting and could enjoy the fan's blast on his bare chest. It was only then that he remembered he had decided to drive down to the port after his siesta to speak to Fiol and since there would be a perfectly legitimate reason for his absence from the office, there was no need to rush.

'Are you all right?' Dolores shouted.

He hesitated. If he declared himself to be feeling not very well, he could resume his siesta. But then Dolores would panic. She might have an over-heated idea of a woman's position in life, but her love for the family was all-embracing and however much he sometimes deplored her attitude, he would never willingly do anything to upset her...

'Are you decent?' she demanded loudly on the other side of the door, making him start.

He was wearing underpants only; observing ancient standards, she would regard his dress as highly indecent. 'No.'

'Then what is wrong? Are you ill? Do you need to go to the health centre?'

'Nothing's the matter.'

'Then why haven't you come downstairs?'

'I'm on my way.'

'As is the future. But that never arrives either.'

He finally rolled off the bed and stood. Why had it been ordained that one should labour six days of the week and rest only on the seventh? The other way round would have been far more equitable.

He climbed the stairs to the office in the boatyard and the pert secretary said Fiol was very busy, but she thought he would be able to speak briefly to the inspector. Alvarez walked through to the inner room, where Fiol was reading a newspaper. 'Your secretary said you were very busy,' Alvarez remarked sarcastically.

'A man in this business has to know what's happening in the world.' Fiol put the paper down.

'So tell me.'

'Tell you what?'

'What's happening in the world.'

198

'Stock markets are going up, so there'll be more money spent on boats and I won't starve, provided I'm not prevented from working by being hounded by someone who's nothing better to do than waste my time.'

Alvarez sat in front of the desk.

'Do feel at home.'

'Then I'll have a coñac.'

'There's no liquor here.'

'As close as ever.'

'I've given up drinking.'

'And I can walk on water.'

'The doctor couldn't give me another three years if I didn't pack it in.'

'And you decided to disappoint everyone? ... Doctors are a miserable bunch, always telling a man what he musn't do. Just like women, wouldn't you say? Or wouldn't you, since the talk is you're a busy man.'

'Who's saying what?' Fiol demanded angrily.

'I never listen to gossip.'

'Then how d'you know the bastards are saying lies about me? I'm faithful to my wife.'

'Then you're getting old and not as strong as you used to be.'

'What the hell d'you want this time?'

'The answers to questions.'

'Ask 'em and clear off.'

'You've told me Señor Rook entertained

199

women on his boat and at least one of 'em was married.'

'And you said you were going to forget it.'

'Until I couldn't. I asked you what her name was and you said you didn't know.'

'Unlike you, I don't take an unhealthy interest in other people's lives.'

'You're certain you don't know what her name is?'

'You don't understand Mallorquin?'

'Then perhaps you can remember something which will help me identify her.'

'And if I don't give a damn whether you do or don't?'

'I'll begin to think you're deliberately annoying me.'

Fiol swore at length, but without imagination. 'All I can tell you is, she drives a Škoda estate.'

'Why would you remember that?'

'You think I'm lying?'

'Probably not, since there's nothing to be gained and a lot to be lost if you are.'

'It was the same as ... as a friend's car.'

'What colour?'

'Silver.'

'Is there anything more you can tell me?'

'No.'

'You've carried out work on Señor Rook's boat, so you know there's a length of rail at the stern which can be lifted out when someone wants to go aboard or ashore.'

'We've been through all this the last time you bothered me.'

'And now we're going to go through it again. Did he ask you to repair the length of rail?'

'If he had, I'd have told you.'

'It would have been a very small job to straighten out the lug, so maybe he spoke to one of the lads and it was done there and then and there was no need to tell you or the foreman about it.'

'You've a funny idea how a successful business is run. I make certain I always know what every hand whose wages I pay is doing.'

'All the same, I'd like to check whether somebody working here was asked to straighten the lug.'

'You can forget the idea.'

'It wouldn't take any time.'

'That's right, it won't, because it's not going to happen and cost me lost work.'

'It's important.'

'That's your problem.'

'Which I thought you'd like to help me with since I'm keen to help you with yours.'

'Any problem that comes my way at work, you'd be as much use as a spoonful of gnat's pee.'

'I wasn't thinking of your work. More that life changes and seldom for the better.'

'When they took you into the Cuerpo it dropped to the floor.'

'Now, a wife goes to court and complains her husband's wandering into other pastures and instead of being told to return home and cook better meals, she's awarded a divorce. Wouldn't matter if the wife wasn't given half the property as well as the divorce. So you'll have a problem if your wife ever comes to hear about that luxury flat in Playa Neuva and Lucía who lives in it. You could end up a poor man.'

'Are you saying that if I won't ... You're a complete bastard!'

'I'm happy I'm not an incomplete one. Shall we go down and talk to the men and find out if any of them can help?'

Thirty-five minutes later, Alvarez left the building and returned to his car. He settled behind the wheel. Since he'd learned nothing, he was going to have to question every ship chandler, every workshop in the port and Llueso capable of doing the work. And if these enquiries proved negative, he would have to extend the area of the search until it made a man weak just to think about the work involved.

Back in his office, he switched on the fan, slumped down in his chair, and closed his eyes to enjoy a brief moment of relaxation. When he awoke, he dialled Palma and asked Vehicles to provide the names and addresses of the owners of silver Škoda estates. No, he did not have a registration number or know the age of the car in question. And yes, he did realize his lack of information was presenting the department with a great deal of extra work, but it was a very important case, the superior chief insisted that the information be provided quickly, and surely in an age of computers ... No, he knew nothing about computers...

He replaced the receiver. In an hour, give or take a few minutes, it would be time to stop work and return home. Did he start questioning ship chandlers and workshops now? Might not Vehicles ring back with the information and if he were not in the office to receive that...

The urbanización, the first to be dedicated in the area, had been built within two hundred metres of the bay, soon after the tourist invasion had begun. The bungalows, mostly in 300-square-metre plots, were small and box-like. Designed as holiday homes, they had cost so little there had been no difficulty in selling them; in the intervening years, their poor workmanship had become obvious, but even so, they were now valued at many times what they had originally cost.

Alvarez parked his car, climbed on to the narrow, uneven pavement, opened the low metal gate and walked up the path which bisected an impoverished lawn of pocket-handkerchief size. There was a bell to the right of the door and he rang this, then turned and stared at other bungalows along the curving road. Although there were signs of life everywhere – people, cars, drying costumes, raised sun umbrellas, patio chairs and tables set outside – when he could remember the area as covered in typical garriga with many evergreen oaks and wild orchids in one favoured spot and very occasionally one could catch a fleeting glimpse of a marauding genet, then to him the area had now become a modern desert. One more example of the destruction wrought by tourism.

The door opened and a man, wearing shirt and baggy shorts, said, 'Yes?' in a voice which lacked any authority.

'Señor Milne?'

'That's me.'

'I am Inspector Alvarez of the Cuerpo General de Policia.'

'Oh!' The exclamation suggested uneasiness as well as surprise.

'I should like to speak to you.'

'But what ... I mean, why?'

'If I might come inside and explain?'

'Yes, of course.'

He stepped into a narrow, carpeted passage on the left-hand wall of which were four framed Dawson prints of square-riggers at sea.

Milne spoke quickly and nervously. 'We'll go out to the patio, if that's all right? It's a bit cooler there than in the house. Such a terribly hot year, isn't it? Someone said it's the hottest on record.'

Alvarez followed Milne out to the small patio at the rear of the house, which was backed by a patch of garden in need of weeding. The only view was of the crests of mountains visible above the roof of the next bungalow. Two deckchairs were by a glass-topped patio table and in one sat a blonde, attractive in catwalk style, who, even seated, had the figure to promote a man's imagination.

Milne made the introduction. 'My wife.'

'Good morning, señora,' Alvarez said. Allowing for a woman's art, she was still considerably younger than her husband. An indication he had found the home of the Škoda which had been seen by Fiol?

'Hullo,' she said, not bothering to sound welcoming.

'He's a policeman,' Milne said. 'Wants to talk to me.'

'What about?'

'I don't know.'

'Wouldn't it be an idea to find out?'

'I thought we'd first come out here, where it's cooler.'

She shrugged her shoulders.

Milne spoke to Alvarez. 'Please sit in that

chair. I'll get another.'

Clearly not a happy home, Alvarez thought as Milne left and he sat. Further confirmation it had been she who had boarded *Corinna*? 'Are you here on holiday, señora?'

'We live here,' she replied sullenly.

Politeness dictated he said something complimentary. 'It's pleasant being so close to the sea.'

'Which is becoming more and more polluted and the beach more packed with people.'

If the beach were empty, she'd probably complain about the solitude.

Milne returned and set up the deckchair he had brought with him. 'It's a little early, perhaps, but can we offer you something to drink?'

Too early? The English had some strange ideas. 'Thank you, señor. Perhaps I might have a coñac with just ice?'

'Yes, of course. The only thing is ... Sarah, did you get the drink when you went shopping earlier?'

'You know I didn't go out.'

'Of course you didn't. Then I'll just see what we have.' He hurried back into the house.

'Do you enjoy the swimming?' Alvarez asked.

'What do you want to talk to Colin about?'

'I have some questions to ask him; and

perhaps you also, señora.'

'But what about?'

'I am investigating the unfortunate death of Señor Rook.'

She looked quickly at him, then away. 'How can that have anything to do with us? Anyway, wasn't it an accident?'

'That is what I have to determine.'

'But if...' She stopped.

Milne returned, a tin tray in his right hand. 'Happily, there was enough brandy for a drink, inspector.' He passed a glass across.

It was a gross exaggeration to call that a drink. 'Thank you, señor.'

Milne passed his wife a glass, put the tray down on the table, picked up the remaining glass, sat. 'Now, what's this all about?' he asked with false confidence.

'As I have just mentioned to the señora, I am investigating the death of Señor Rook because it is not yet certain that it was an accident.'

'You're suggesting he was killed by someone?'

'It is possible.'

'Good God!'

'You are surprised?'

'Of course I am.'

'I am sorry. I do not speak English as well as I should wish and perhaps my question was obscure. Are you surprised not by his death, but by the fact someone might have wanted to kill him?'

'I'm not certain I appreciate the difference.'

'He's asking you if you ever imagined anyone could dislike him sufficiently to want to kill him,' she said sharply.

'If I'd ever thought about it, maybe *I* would.'

'Don't be so damned silly!'

'Steady on, sweet.'

'Stop talking like that.' She turned to Alvarez. 'My husband thinks it's amusing to try to sound smart.'

'I'm not trying to do anything but answer the question,' he said quietly, but with conviction.

There was the hint, if no more, of a stronger character than the diffident manner would suggest, Alvarez thought. Yet if that were so, why did he allow her to treat him with open contempt? 'Señor, why would you consider it possible someone might have wished to kill him?'

'Because of his lifestyle.'

'In what way?'

'He was arrogant and set out to get what he wanted.'

'What did he want?'

'Other people's money and wives.'

'You're becoming ridiculous,' she snapped.

'Ask Derek for his opinion.'

'He was a fool.'

208

'Because he was naive enough to trust Maurice?'

'It makes me sick, hearing you talk like that.'

Milne picked up his glass and drank.

'Why would he have to be naive?' Alvarez asked.

'What's it matter?' Milne put his glass down on the table.

'I will have to know all I can about Señor Rook's life before I can be certain.'

'Certain about what?'

'Whether, or not, he was murdered.'

'I thought you said he was.'

'That it is possible. Just as it is possible his death was an accident. So now please tell me why Señor Carr was naive.'

'I don't think I'll answer that.'

She said, speaking with contempt: 'My husband thinks he's still in the fifth form and there's no sneaking on pain of being tarred and feathered. Maurice persuaded Derek to join in some form of development in Andalucía and that went sour, so Derek lost all his money. So now, he and Vivien don't know how they're going to survive.'

'But he wouldn't...' Milne stopped.

'Wouldn't what, señor?'

'He'd never have done anything physical.'

'What makes you so sure?' she demanded.

'What are you suggesting?'

'Only that when someone's as worried as

he's been, there's no real knowing what he'll do.'

Without subtlety or thought to the consequences, Alvarez judged, she was trying to direct his mind because then he might not bother about, or even become aware of, Rook's sexual affairs.

She stood. 'If that's everything, I've some shopping to do.'

'Señora, would you be kind enough to wait a few moments?' Alvarez asked.

'Why?'

'I have some more questions.'

'My husband can answer them.'

'I should prefer you both to do so.'

Reluctantly, she sat.

Alvarez spoke to Milne. 'You seemed to suggest Señor Rook was friendly with married women?'

'Because he will listen to the filthy rumours people enjoy spreading,' she snapped.

'You believe they are only rumours?'

'The locals only had to see him talking to a woman and they'd claim he was chasing her and she wasn't running. He was handsome, rich, amusing, so naturally all the stolid, boring people made up stories to boost themselves by denigrating him. Anyway, what does it matter?'

'A jealous husband, señora, can be a dangerous man.'

'You think the husbands here have any balls?'

Had she realized she was looking at Milne when she had spoken so fiercely? 'Do you think Señor Rook may have had an affair with someone's wife?'

'When Gloria was around? She'd very quickly scotch that idea.'

'It has been suggested to me that he did so when she was abroad.'

'I keep telling you, it's the small, mean little people who spread those calumnies.'

Alvarez turned. 'Señor, what car do you own?'

'Why on earth do you want to know that?'

'It may be of some importance.'

'Damned if I can think why ... It's a Škoda estate.'

'And its colour?'

'Silver.' He turned to face Sarah. 'Have you had some sort of an accident?'

'Of course I haven't,' she answered shrilly.

'Do you often drive to the marina, señor?'

'Very seldom, if ever.'

Alvarez turned to Sarah. 'And you, señora, do you often drive to the marina?'

'No.'

He saw – or thought he did – fear in her eyes because she could guess where his questions were now leading. She would only experience fear if there were cause – she had boarded *Corrina* with Rook and sailed into a sea of passion. If the questions were pressed now, she would try to evade direct and honest answers, but in doing so, she would probably betray herself to Milne. However much he might condemn her for cuckolding her husband, he did not want to be responsible for exposing this. If she were to suffer for her disloyalty, let it be at the hands of someone else.

He looked at his watch. 'I have to leave.' He drained his glass – easily done – put it on the table and stood. 'You may well remember,' he said, looking at Sarah, 'something which will help me reach the truth; if that is so, please come and see me at the guardia post in the village. That will avoid my having to return and ask more questions which you may well find annoying.' He hoped she had the wit to understand what he was not saying.

Milne came to his feet. 'You shouldn't ... That is, I suggest you don't take any notice of the gossip. Some of the ex-pats have very loose tongues.'

He accompanied Alvarez to the front door. Alvarez stepped out, stopped. 'There is one last question. Do you own a boat?'

'Do we look as if we have a fifty-foot ketch in the marina?' Milne had tried to speak ironically, but succeeding only in sounding petulant.

The Ibiza was like an oven. Alvarez

lowered the front windows and switched on the fan, bemoaning the lack of air-conditioning as he did so. If one assumed Rook had been murdered, the murderer must either have been aboard when *Corrina* left or he had sailed out to meet it – her – at sea. Even if Milne had the strongest of motives for murder – certainty of his wife's adultery – would he have acted? He was a weak man, with only a hint of any inner strength. Yet a weak man might commit murder when half crazed from jealousy and humiliation.

He drove to the entrance of the urbanización and waited for several cars to pass. What would Salas say if he ever learned one of his inspectors had not faced a possible suspect with the facts because of a sense of compassion?

Nineteen

Alvarez drove slowly up the short, steep access to the second lateral road of the urbanizacíon; above this was one more road along which were houses, built on a slope, which only foreigners would have considered. Some of the larger properties were said to be worth over a hundred and sixty million pesetas (or roughly a million euros, if one wished to calculate in that obnoxious currency). If he had been told thirty years before that any property other than a possessió could be worth so much, he would have considered the speaker a fool or a conman. That there were so many people able to pay a fortune for a house was an insight into his own impoverishment.

He braked to a halt by a gateway set in a dry-stone wall. On the right-hand pillar was a nameplate – Ca'n Derek. Another foreigner who did not understand that when naming properties, the Mallorquins used nicknames, not given names. The house, not one of the largest, but not small, lay five metres below the level of the road. He decided to leave his car on the road – brakes might fail, steering might lock, suspension might collapse, the stricken car might veer to the right of the garage and plunge on to the sloping rock, turn over and over...

His walk down was made easier by the rope handrail, yet he reached the flat area with relief and aware of the muscles in the back of his legs. The front door was panelled in traditional style and had a small inspection port protected by a grille. He rang the bell. A dog began to bark. The port opened and a man said, 'Yes?' in English.

'Inspector Alvarez, Cuerpo de Policia.'

The port shut. The door opened to reveal a man in his early seventies, face heavily lined, expression lugubrious. He suddenly shouted, 'No,' causing Alvarez to start, then bent down and picked up a Border terrier which was eager to greet the visitor and, since its mouth was open to reveal a fine set of teeth, perhaps to enjoy a playful bite.

'Don't worry,' Carr said in halting Spanish, 'he is very good.'

But good at what?

'Who is it?' a woman called out.

'A policeman,' Carr replied.

A woman stepped into the doorway at the far end of the rectangular hall. She addressed Alvarez in reasonable Spanish. 'Is there a problem?'

She had a pleasant face, but one that would be difficult to recall in detail because features melded into each other; she was not quite fat and was dressed in a cheerfully patterned frock which was comfortable at the expense of style; her manner was direct. The kind of Englishwoman, he judged, who would always be prepared to wield a handbag. 'I am investigating the death of Señor Rook, señora, and it is possible you may be able to help me.'

She spoke to her husband. 'You can put Isis down.'

'I thought it best—'

'He'll be all right.'

As Alvarez stepped into the hall, Carr put Isis down on the floor. Isis advanced and sniffed Alvarez's trousers, wagged his tail.

'You like dogs,' she said approvingly.

Since it seemed he was not to be savaged, he agreed he liked dogs. To underline his assertion, he bent down and patted Isis's head, hoping thereby to earn her approval and co-operation. As was well known, English women preferred their dogs to their husbands.

'Will you come this way.'

He followed her into the sitting room. 'You have a wonderful situation, señora,' he said, as he looked through the picture window at the view of the distant bay and encircling mountains.

'We like it.'

He noted that her tone had been bitter, not

appreciative.

'Do sit.'

He settled on one of the comfortable arm-chairs, she on another. Carr remained standing. Isis came up to Alvarez, was called back, jumped up on to her lap.

'Are we allowed to offer you a drink?' Carr asked.

Alvarez tried to understand the question.

Observing his puzzlement, Carr said: 'At home, a policeman doesn't drink when on duty.'

Most countries suffered strange customs. 'It is left to our discretion, señor, and I should very much welcome a drink.'

'So what would you like?'

'May I have a coñac with just ice?'

'Of course.' Carr spoke to his wife. 'The usual for you?'

'Yes, please.'

Carr left the room. Vivien fondled Isis's ear as she said: 'Since you're investigating Maurice's death, it may not have been an accident?'

'We do not yet know for certain whether it was or was not an accident.'

'But he was shot?'

'No, señora.'

'That's what people are saying.'

'He suffered a blow to the head which caused him to fall into the sea and he un-fortunately drowned. The cause of the blow

217

may well have been that the boat was moving unevenly and he lost his balance and struck his head as he fell.'

'Then why have you come here to ask us questions?'

'I have to consider all possibilities.'

'Such as?'

He did not answer.

'For some reason you think we can help you?'

'I am talking to several people in the hope I learn something which will enable me to determine the truth.'

'You're questioning everyone who knew him?'

'To many who did, señora.'

'But not everyone. So you obviously reckon we are more likely than others to be able to help you. Why's that? What places us on your priority list?'

'There is no such list.'

'Isn't that being tactful rather than accurate?'

Carr, carrying a tray, returned. He handed out the glasses, sat. 'Your health, inspector.'

Alvarez drank. It was cheap brandy.

'Maurice wasn't shot,' she said to her husband.

'So rumour's as inaccurate as ever.'

'He received some sort of a blow to the head which knocked him into the sea, too dazed to save himself.'

'Then how can we say anything that's relevant?'

'A question I've asked, but the inspector has not answered.'

Carr turned to Alvarez. 'If it was an accident, why are you here?'

'Because I cannot be certain it was an accident, señor.'

'I don't understand.'

'As I have said to the señora, the blow may have been as a result of Señor Rook's falling as the boat moved unevenly and he lost his balance. But as there is no certainty this was the case, I have to consider the alternative.'

'Which is?'

'That someone hit him.'

'It's beginning to seem as if...' Carr became silent.

'As if we might know what happened,' she said.

'Señora, all I am trying to do is to establish the facts.'

'And that, surely, would be the most important one?'

She was too sharp for a woman. Alvarez spoke to Carr. 'I understand you entered in a business arrangement with Señor Rook?'

'Rushed, not entered.' She spoke harshly.

'And this arrangement proved unsuccessful?'

'Catastrophic for us.'

'He didn't know the autonomous government was going to allow another developer to pinch the land—' Carr began.

'Didn't he always boast how smart he was? I'll bet he understood the possibility and just took the risk.'

'He can't have done. He lost a great deal more money than I did.'

'That's what he told you. The only money he really lost was yours.'

'Señora,' Alvarez said, 'he was speaking the truth. He did lose a very considerable sum of money.'

'Good!'

'My wife ... My wife is upset because of what's happened,' Carr said, as if that were not obvious.

'Is that surprising?' she demanded. 'I've been wonderfully happy here until you wouldn't understand what kind of a man Maurice was.'

'The scheme sounded so promising...'

'Does a con-man succeed in fooling his victim by telling the truth?'

'We needed the money...'

'Because you kept sending more and more to Tim.'

'He was so worried about all his debts...'

'Why the hell should we have to pay for Vera's extravagances?' She came to her feet. 'How could you have let him ruin our lives?' She hurried out of the room. Isis followed her.

Carr cleared his throat. 'I'm sorry about that, inspector.'

'There's nothing to apologize for, señor.'

'She's very upset because we're having to sell the house.' He drained his glass. 'Maurice was so certain the development would be a success and I thought ... Tim, our son, is in the navy and doing rather well. But his wife ... She's from a very wealthy family and has never learned to economize. If she wants something, she buys it without a thought of where the money's to come from. Tim wrote and said their debts had become so large, they were beginning to threaten his career. That so upset Vivien that when I heard Maurice talking about all the money he was going to make ... God knows where it's all going to end.'

In disaster, Alvarez thought. Life delighted in kicking a man when he was down. 'Do you own a boat, señor?'

'No. And if I did, it would be up for sale. Why the hell didn't I listen to Vivien, not him?'

'Did he actively encourage you to invest in his scheme?'

'On the contrary. He said he didn't advise my joining in with him – which, because I'm a bloody fool, made me all the more insistent to do so.'

Alvarez stood. 'Thank you for your help, señor.'

Vivien, with Isis, returned. 'Are you off?' And if you aren't, why not? 'Yes, señora.'

He left the house and slowly made his way up the steep drive, sweating and short of breath. Like Milne, Carr did not appear to be of a character to commit murder. But a wife could warp a man's character.

The internal phone rang as Alvarez decided it was still too early to leave the post and return home for a drink and supper. He lifted the receiver. 'Yes?'

'Someone's here who wants a word with you.'

'Who?'

'Señora Milne.'

'I'll be down.'

'Moving faster than you have in years!'

But not for the reason the salacious cabo thought.

He went down and across to where Sarah Milne was waiting. 'Good evening, señora.'

She spoke in a small, nervous voice. 'I thought ... It seemed to be a good idea to come...' She stopped.

'Shall we go up to my room where there'll be more privacy?' His words were meant to snub the cabo's inquisitive interest, but having spoken, he realized they were capable of a wrong interpretation.

In his room, he moved a chair in front of the desk, altered the fan to allow her a share of the benefit of the draught, sat. Despite obviously being in a very distraught state of mind, she remained warmly, naively attractive. One imagined her on a grassy hill, bathed in sunshine, singing; she prompted thoughts of slaying a modern dragon to gain her approval; she would encourage a man to honour honour ... Which was all nonsense because she and Rook ... 'Do you smoke, señora?'

'No ... No, thank you.'

'Do you mind if I do?'

She began to pluck the edge of her small handbag. 'You said...' She stopped.

He lit a cigarette. 'Señora, before we proceed, perhaps I should know if your husband is aware you have come here to speak to me?'

She looked down at her handbag. 'No,' she said.

'Then I will not mention the fact to him.'

Through the opened window, but closed shutters, came the noise of the road – traffic, speech in many languages which combined into a low babel.

'You said that if there were anything I had forgotten to tell you...'

'It was your car which was parked near *Corrina*, wasn't it? And it was you who boarded the boat?'

'Yes, but ... It's not what it seems. Maurice had asked me if I'd like to go for a sail. I love the sea and ... It was a chance to enjoy myself and there wasn't any harm in it. People with nasty minds might think ... But all we did was go beyond the bay, have a drink and a picnic.'

'You only went on this one voyage?'

'Yes.'

'Did you ever go on the boat when it stayed in the harbour?'

'Of course not.'

'Are you sure?'

'Yes.'

'You must know, señora, I have spoken to people who say they have seen you more than once go aboard *Corrina* when it did not sail.'

'They're lying,' she said with the anger of fear. 'Why should I do that?'

'I am hoping you have come here to tell me.'

'I came here to try and help. I didn't know you'd be making filthy suggestions.'

'Señora, I have suggested nothing.'

'I know what you're thinking.'

'I rather doubt that.'

'You think I was having an affair with Maurice. I wasn't,' she said violently. She stood. 'I'm not staying to be insulted.'

'I am sorry if you think I have in any way insulted you.'

'How do you imagine I feel when ... when...'

'Señora, in my job I unfortunately have

sometimes to be suspicious and there is always a great pleasure when I learn my suspicions are unfounded. Therefore, I would ask you to remain and answer a few more questions so that I can discount any thoughts I may now have.'

'I won't stay here.'

'That is a pity since it means I will have to speak to you again in your own house and your husband may be present. I am certain some of my questions will not be welcomed by him.'

She slowly sat. She rested her elbows on the arms of the chair, her outstretched fingers on her forehead as if suffering from a severe headache.

'I need to know the truth.'

'I ... I've told you.'

'Did you ever go aboard *Corrina* when it stayed in harbour?'

After a moment, she nodded.

'Did you visit Son Raldo when Señora Rook was not there?'

'Only once and he wasn't on his own – all the staff were there.'

'The staff have told me it was more than once.'

'I can't help what they say.'

'They also say that if you were there, they had orders to keep to their own accommodation.'

'Why won't you understand they're lying?'

'Staff can be very inquisitive and when they are given unusual orders, they like to find out why ... Earlier, I told you I needed the truth because I am investigating the death of Señor Rook. If I think you are lying to me, I will have to find out why.'

She removed her elbows from the arms of the chair, folded them in front of herself, stared fixedly to the right of Alvarez. 'It wasn't an affair. We just ... once or twice ... Please, please don't tell my husband.'

'I have already said there should be no need to do that.'

'He ... he can be so jealous.'

'Does he know?'

'Of course not.'

'Might he suspect?'

'Only because ... Leslie's a nasty little man who loves causing trouble. He told Colin I'd been at Son Raldo when Gloria was abroad.'

'You had not told your husband of your visit?'

'I didn't think ... Oh, God, if only...'

If only – the two most useless words in any language. 'Did your husband ask you why you'd visited Son Raldo?'

'He went on and on about it.'

'You persuaded him your visit was of no significance?'

Her tone was defensive. 'You don't understand.'

That was true. A married man sometimes

needed to enjoy himself; a married woman should remain faithful.

'Colin is so ... so boring.'

And older than she, and far less wealthy than Rook. Alvarez silently sighed. Inequality was a fact of life, yet who could judge the pain it caused? 'Thank you for coming here and telling me what you have, señora.'

'You won't say a word to my husband?'

'As I have already mentioned, he will not hear it from me.'

She seemed about to say something more, but did not. She stood, hurriedly crossed to the door and left. By the time he reached the head of the stairs, she was at the foot. Since there was little point in his following her, he returned to his room, sat, decided he might as well have a drink before he left and returned home for drinks and the meal. As he poured himself a man-size measure, he pondered the question, what degree of jealousy would drive a man of Milne's character to violence?

Twenty

On Thursday morning, Alvarez parked in front of an unfinished building – roof, floors, but only outside walls, never finished to save rates, owned by the four beneficiaries of their father's will who had disagreed for thirty years as to whether there was more benefit to be gained from a sale today or the increasing value of a sale tomorrow.

The open ground floor was rented by a small metal-working firm. He went in and, shouting because a man was hammering a metal sheet for no immediately apparent reason, asked if they had straightened the lug of a section of boat's rail for Señor Rook? They hadn't. He left, glad to escape the noise, checked the time. It was past merienda time. He walked up the recently pedestrianized road to the old square and Club Llueso.

'Don't tell me, I'll guess,' the bartender said. 'You're late because you forgot to wake up and now you'd like a coffee and a small coñac.'

'Wrong on both counts. I'm late because

I've been working and I want a coffee and a large coñac.'

'You know, Enrique, if you're not careful, your liver will seize up.'

'Not all the time I keep it well oiled.'

Alvarez crossed to one of the window tables and thankfully sat. It had been a very busy and frustrating morning. He'd questioned one ship chandler and two metal-working firms, he'd asked two of the three firms in the port which chartered boats if Milne or Carr had hired one recently, and he'd learned nothing. Yet until he could find where the rail had been repaired and whether or not it had been returned, it was likely to be all but impossible to determine the nature of Rook's death.

The bartender came across to the table and put cup, saucer, and glass down. 'You're looking even more worn-out than usual.'

'Because I can't seem to have a moment without somebody interrupting me and making impertinent comments.'

'Then you'd better make certain it doesn't happen again and carry your order from the bar to the table.' As the bartender walked away, Alvarez brought a pack of cigarettes out of his pocket. A reduction of smoking did not mean abstention. He lit a cigarette. He drank some brandy, poured what remained in the glass into the coffee. 'You can give me another coñac,' he called out.

'And you can fetch it.'

The concept of service had largely become a forgotten one.

There was as yet nothing to decide whether Rook's death had been murder or accident, so which, logically, was the more likely? When there were three persons with strong motives for wishing him dead, surely murder? But one could possess a strong motive for murder, yet never commit it because of a belief in the sanctity of life, fear of the law and the consequences of breaking it...

He finished the brandy, looked across at the bar and saw the well-filled glass which stood on it. Did he ask the bartender to bring it to the table and risk a robust and insolent refusal or did he suffer a diminution of authority and get it? Decisions, decisions. He stood, carried the empty glass to the bar and was annoyed when the bartender mockingly smiled. He would find another bar at which to enjoy his meriendas. But another bartender might not have such a generous pouring hand...

He sat. As he finished the brandy, he came to a decision. After lunch – that was, after his siesta – he'd pursue with even greater energy his attempt to find out if the rail had been repaired and returned; if necessary, he'd even work well into the evening.

★ ★ ★

After the siesta and hot chocolate and two slices of coca, he drove down to the port. He questioned the staff of another ship chandler. They had known Señor Rook, but he had never asked them to arrange the repair of a section of boat's rail. He spoke to the Frenchman on the beach who hired catamarans by the hour to tourists – the Frenchman had not been approached by Rook. He spoke to the owner of a shop which, amongst other things, sold a certain amount of boats' gear. Who was Señor Rook?

He became gloomily certain he was faced by a task equal to that of the ancient who had had to push a block of marble up towards the crest of a hill, only to have it roll back every time...

'A penny for them.'

He looked up to face Gail.

'Are all the cares of the world weighing down your shoulders?' she asked.

'Almost all of them. But if you'll have a coffee with me, I'll be able to forget them for a while.'

'How could I refuse so gallant an invitation? Or is it a double-edged one? You have still more questions?'

'That is not why I suggested coffee.'

'Then I was wrong to think perhaps my company had become unwelcome?'

'How could you possibly imagine that?'

'You don't remember?'

He wanted to ask what he was supposed to remember, but her mischievous smile convinced him she would not give a straight answer.

'Come on, Enrique, tell the truth and shame the devil. You have completely forgotten.'

Forgotten what? ... As if a bolt of lightning had struck nearby, he was shocked by the thought that he had not pursued his recent invitation to a meal. The pressure of work could addle a man's brains. 'I haven't been able to get through to you on the phone.' Which in one sense was true. Her quick smile worried him. 'As a matter of fact...' He hoped she was not of the same opinion as Dolores. '...I was going to drive over to Son Raldo later on this evening to find out if you'd like to go out.'

'Yes, please.'

'When?'

'For fear the phone will once again go kaput, why not this evening?'

'Shall I pick you up at around nine?'

'I'll be waiting. And please let's go somewhere this time that's not all tarted up for the tourists, where the food is genuine Mallorquin and not chips with everything. Or is there nowhere left like that?'

'There is a restaurant I know which hasn't changed in fifty years, but there is a problem.'

'I'm quite sure you're someone who has a problem if there isn't a problem. What is this one?'

'The cooking is good. The llenguardo amb bolets could grace a king's table.'

'And if it did, what would the king be looking at?'

'Sole with mushrooms.'

'I love sole, so let's forget the problem.'

'But the restaurant is only used by ordinary Mallorquins who want value for money and they can be a little rough in their manners; the ambience is very rustic.'

'One eats with one's fingers?'

'We've never done that. Not for hundreds of years, anyway.'

She briefly touched his arm. 'It's wonderful the way you leap to defend the island and everyone and everything on it because you're so proud of your heritage. I wish the British were allowed to be as proud of their country without politically correct idiots terming that racism.'

He silently swore. How could he have been so solid as not to appreciate the joke? He suggested, despite their exorbitant prices, that they had coffee at one of the front cafés. As they walked, he was so conscious of her presence that he failed to note the two young women who were sunbathing in monokinis of extraordinary fragility.

★ ★ ★

Alvarez walked into the sitting room, sat, reached across the table and picked up the bottle of brandy, poured himself a drink, added four cubes of ice from the insulated container.

'You're back late,' Jaime said.

'I've more work than two could handle.' He looked at his watch. An hour before he should leave to drive to Son Raldo.

'So what's keeping you so busy?'

'Trying to decide whether the Englishman died from an accident on his boat or was murdered.'

'Since he was a foreigner, who's bothered?'

'His wife maybe is.'

'You said he was rich. So she inherits everything and starts to spend.'

Dolores swept through the bead curtain and stood with arms folded. 'So! My husband thinks a wife is not bothered when her husband dies?'

'What I meant was—' Jaime began.

'And doubtless is convinced a husband is never happier than when his wife dies.'

'Why say that?'

'If you haven't already chosen my successor, I suggest you proceed carefully. Make certain she is a good cook because you are more concerned with your own pleasures than anyone else's. She must be content to watch you drink until the few words you are capable of speaking are nonsense. She must understand that if there is work to be done, it is useless to ask you to do it.'

'All I said was—'

'Of course, I am wasting my breath. What man released from the unwanted presence of a wife who has spent her life slaving to serve him, ever chooses wisely? Like a child beguiled by a cheap but colourful toy, he chooses a woman who is young and pretty because in his stupidity he believes she flatters his image. Aiyee! When the Good Lord decided there should be men as well as women on this earth, He made a mistake.' She returned into the kitchen.

'All I said was, this woman will probably find herself another husband. What's wrong with that?' Jaime asked plaintively.

'It was the way you said it.' Alvarez was annoyed. The last thing he wanted was Dolores in a bad mood.

'I said it like I say everything else.'

'Which is why your words were so objectionable,' came the call from the kitchen.

Jaime finished his drink, regarded the bottle.

Dolores came through the bead curtain. 'When my mother used to tell me a woman who married sacrificed herself, a man who married sacrificed his wife, I did not fully understand what she meant. Unfortunately, now I do. I have slaved all day in the kitchen, despite the heat and the fan, which will not work properly because my husband can never find time away from drinking to mend it, preparing, because I know my cousin likes it so much, estofat de xot.' She waited for their delighted surprise.

Alvarez, understanding how a Christian had felt just before he was pushed into the arena to amuse a lion, said: 'As a matter of fact...'

'What untruth do you wish to tell me now?'

For one ignominious moment, he considered phoning Gail to cancel their meal. Courage returned. 'I'm afraid I have to go out this evening.' He picked up his glass and drained it.

'Indeed!'

He refilled his glass.

'Is one permitted to know why you wish to leave before you eat?'

'I don't want to go, but very important work has turned up and must be dealt with immediately.'

'As there has been no phone call since you came in, you knew about this work before you returned home. Yet you were unable to tell me until now?'

'I didn't know you were cooking something special.'

'My cooking is usually so ordinary it can be dismissed without a second thought?'

'Your cooking is always superb.'

'As my mother all too often had to remark, a man's praise is genuine only when it concerns himself. This work is very urgent?'

'Otherwise I wouldn't dream of leaving before the meal.'

'Yet it is not so urgent that you can sit and drink?'

'I can't start the work for another half hour.'

'Because she won't be ready?'

'What do you mean?'

'As if I could believe you would miss my estofat de xot on account of work! You think I have the mind of a weak and feeble man?' She turned and went through the bead curtain with such energy that for some time afterwards the long strings clashed against each other. A saucepan was banged with considerable force.

The restaurant was in one of the back streets of Port Llueso and from the outside could not have been less inviting; one of the panes of glass in the right-hand window had been broken and the replacement – a square of cardboard – had obviously been in place for a long time; the list of dishes behind an almost opaque plastic cover was illegibly written only in Mallorquin. Inside was no more prepossessing. Ten square tables were set with paper place-mats; the olives were home prepared and would shrivel a mouth unprepared for them and the slices of bara were in ancient, stained wicker baskets; there might, or might not, be condiments in place; the service was friendly, but slow; on the walls were ancient, faded, even torn bull-fighting posters featuring as the main matador Miguel Ríos – for the owner of the restaurant, a greater matador than Belmonte had ever been...

There was loud laughter and talk as Gail and Alvarez entered, then there was silence as the dozen men, at various tables, stared at them.

The only waiter limped up to the table – his right leg was shorter than his left, following a fall whilst trying to break into a villa. 'You want to eat?' His tone was surly. Women were barely tolerated, foreign women actively discouraged.

'What d'you think we want?' Alvarez replied in coarse Mallorquin.

'A quick one,' called out a bearded man, with the build of a rugger player. 'And from the look of you, that's all you're good for.'

'And your dish is what? A plump young boy?'

There was laughter. Emilio was always boasting about his conquests amongst the female tourists.

'I've a mind to shove your teeth down your throat.'

'And I'm wondering if you did the

jewellers in Carrer Padre Roca a couple of months back?'

'You think I'd touch the crap they sell?'

'You might have moved up the scale.'

There was more laughter, some of it sycophantic. Several of the men were old enough to remember times when a policeman had to be treated with respect if one wished to lead a peaceful life.

Alvarez spoke uncertainly to Gail. 'Perhaps I shouldn't have suggested we came here.'

'For heaven's sake,' she replied, 'it's just what I hoped; like losing fifty years and all the tourists. Was that man being very rude to you?'

'He was trying to be.'

'But you were ruder back? What did you say?'

'I've forgotten.'

'It was that awful? Before the night's out, you're going to tell me.'

What else would he tell her?

Twenty-one

Alvarez parked in front of No. 7, one of twenty-three one-floor terraced houses whose bleak exteriors, often softened with flower baskets, offered no indication of the comfort to be found inside some of them. Decades before, every one would have been occupied by a fisherman and his family – the road was called Carrer de Festa des pa i des peix – now, many were owned by foreigners.

Riera's house showed neglect – the rendering on the front wall was flaking, the shutters needed repainting, as did the front door which had begun to rot at the foot. Alvarez opened the door and stepped into the entrada which was spotlessly clean, but furnished only with two cane chairs, a Mallorquin chest, a threadbare hemp carpet, and two religious prints depicting Peter and Andrew leaving their nets. He called out and a middle-aged woman, her face lined and leathered from years working in the fields, came through the far doorway. He asked if Riera was at home.

Matilde nodded, turned and left without a word. She had lost the power of speech when young and there had not been the money to pay for the medical attention which might have cured the disability.

Riera, dressed in a rough shirt, drawn tight by broad shoulders, and heavy-duty cotton trousers which had seen much work, entered. 'So it's you! Matilde didn't know you and I reckoned to find some sly bastard trying to sell something. You'd best come through before you tell me what brings you here.'

Alvarez followed the other through a small room and into the kitchen, which still had the large open fireplace in which all the cooking had once been done and around which, in winter, the family had sat for warmth.

Matilde stirred the contents of an earthenware pot on the small gas stove. 'It's Enrique Alvarez,' Riera said.

Her expression and quick smile showed that now he had been named, she recognized him and apologized for not having done so before.

'You'll have a drink?' Riera asked.

Alvarez did not answer immediately. Riera was unable to earn because his boat was unseaworthy, added to which he was in debt; even the giving of basic hospitality must strain his finances. But to refuse a drink because of this would be to humiliate him. 'Just a small one.'

'Growing old?'

'My superior chief may be along later to see how things are running and he holds drink is bad.'

'The world's full of daft sods. You surely don't take any notice of him?'

'I reckon I must.'

'Then you're not only grown old, you've become soft.'

'It happens to all of us.'

'Not to me, it doesn't.'

Which was true, Alvarez thought, as Riera turned and walked across to a row of shelves. Men who worked the sea dared not become soft.

Riera returned and handed Alvarez a glass in which was a brandy as generous as he would have poured himself, was careful not to reveal how much was in his own. They sat on chairs in front of the fireplace, as if seeking heat.

'What's it all about then?' Riera asked.

'Señor Rook,' Alvarez answered.

'That bastard!'

'I'm having to enquire into his death.'

'Who's bothered about that?'

'I am.'

'More fool you.'

'You didn't like him because you were involved in a collision with him?'

'I wasn't involved. It was all that bastard's fault. Because he was in a boat that cost more euros than there are stars in the sky, he reckoned he'd the right of way and expected me to sheer off in my crap little llaüt. He rammed me...'

Alvarez patiently listened as Rook's total lack of seamanship was detailed, how Rook had aggressively refused to accept responsibility, and to the iniquities of insurance companies who were legalized swindlers.

'Did you say you'd teach the bastard the rich can't always get away with everything?'

Riera drank.

'Was it something like that you said to Fiol?'

'Could've been,' he muttered.

'Because you were so angry?'

'I wasn't going to be all smiles, was I?'

'Angry enough to carry out your threat?'

'What's this all about?'

'I have to decide whether Señor Rook accidentally fell over the side and drowned or was helped on his way.'

'And you're thinking...?'

Matilde made a sound which expressed her frightened concern.

'Your words suggest that when you had the chance, you were going to teach Señor Rook he couldn't ram your boat and get away with it.'

'It was talk.'

'Threatening talk.'

'And you're soft enough to think I meant it?'

'Perhaps.'

'Has some lying sod said I did him in?'

'Not yet.'

'Then why come here talking balls?'

'I have to find out if someone had the motive, the strength of mind, and the cunning, to kill Señor Rook and make it appear to be an accident. You had the motive and the will. But cunning? That calls for someone who can smile at you as he gets ready to throttle you...'

'I've never harmed anyone.'

'You made a mess of Sanchez.'

'That's years ago.'

'Pigs don't change their grunt.'

'He tried to make fun of her.' Riera indicated Matilde.

'So you sent him off to hospital.'

'What would you have done?'

'The same as you, I hope.'

'I don't bleeding well understand you.'

'If someone did kill Señor Rook, he had to know how and when to rendezvous with *Corrina*, board it, have some fishing net ready, shove the señor over the side, make certain the net was well and truly wrapped around the propeller, and return to harbour.'

'When did the bastard drown?'

'June the sixteenth.'

'My boat was in Fiol's place.'

'Which wouldn't stop you borrowing a friend's boat for a few hours; a friend who'd

244

keep his mouth as tight shut as a clam.'

'Prove it.'

'Then you did borrow a boat?'

'What d'you mean?'

'Tell me to prove it and there must be something to be proved.'

Riera's anger grew. 'You've always made yourself out to be so bloody smart.'

'You had every reason to hate the señor, so you decided to face him at sea and force him to accept responsibility for the damage to your boat; all he needed to do to help you was refer your claim to his insurers and it would be paid. But being a foreigner, a rich foreigner, he wasn't going to listen to the likes of you and told you to clear off. Being treated like unwanted flotsam made you even angrier and you lost your temper and attacked him, using the removable section of the rail. Or wasn't it like that? Did you threaten him, he backed away, and in his fright fell and banged his head and then, semi-conscious, forgetting the rail was missing because it was being repaired, reached for the support that wasn't there and fell over the back? Did you watch him slowly drift away, unable to decide whether to dive in and save him...'

'I can't bloody swim.'

'You've been at sea all these years and can't swim?'

'What of it?'

'You're either very brave or lack all imagination. But you could have thrown him a life-buoy.'

'When I was ashore?'

'You need to think hard.'

'And that wouldn't do you no harm.'

'The law allows there is a big difference between causing a man's death and watching him die when action you could have taken might have saved him. If you admit you shouted at him, but didn't touch him before he fell—'

'I wasn't at sea because my boat's in the boatyard, I didn't board that bastard's gin palace, didn't threaten him, didn't see him fall over the side. But if I had, I'd have done what I could to save him.'

'When you admit you hated him?'

'If you're a seaman, you'd try to rescue the devil from drowning.'

Alvarez found that difficult to accept, but then he was no seaman.

Twenty-two

'You're to phone the superior chief,' the duty cabo said, as Alvarez entered the post soon after midday.

'What's the panic?'

'Likely it's to find out if you're still alive. None of us could answer that.'

Alvarez walked up to his room, silently bemoaning the loss of respect the young showed their elders and betters. He sat behind the desk. So much had changed since he was young that memories seemed to come from a different world. His father had owned land by the sea; the land had been poor and called for much labour for little return. As the tourist invasion began, a foreigner with a silver tongue had offered to buy his property. No peasant ever willingly forwent a square metre of soil, but eventually the price he was offered became so great compared to what he had ever possessed, he could no longer resist the temptation. What he had been quite unable to realize was that, as the buyer judged, the land would soon become worth many, many times what he was to be paid. The money had quickly disappeared because his father had had no experience in handling what to him had been an almost inexhaustible sum and he had given his wife luxuries for the first time in their married life. He had had to get a job as a farm labourer. Conditions had been hard, but far better than in the days of the roters – men who had had to clear tons of stones and rock from the land before it could be tilled, had had to build primitive dwellings with the stone and rock in which they and their animals had lived – a thin mud wall separating them – and their beds were palliasses on the earth floors, the furniture, home-made...

The phone rang.

'The superior chief will speak to you,' said the plum-voiced secretary.

'What day is it?' Salas demanded.

'Señor?'

'The question is too complicated?'

'It's just that I am surprised that your secretary cannot answer you. But perhaps she did not buy a morning paper and does not have—'

'Have you been drinking?'

'I never drink on duty, señor,' Alvarez said, as he reached down to the bottom right-hand drawer.

'How many days ago did I give you an order?'

248

He poured himself a larger drink than he might otherwise have done, to counter the trouble the question portended.

'Should the fact you cannot answer me not surprise me? Unfortunately, it should not. Your inability to understand your job has not been a matter for surprise for a long time.'

There was another silence.

'Are you still there?' Salas demanded with the sweetness of aloes.

'I was trying to be certain I understood what you said, señor.'

'I could not have expressed myself more clearly. The insolence of you Mallorquins never fails to astound me.'

'I wasn't trying to be insolent.'

'Then for once your lack of effort has achieved success.'

'You mentioned so many negatives and I was wondering if two negatives make a positive when one is speaking as well as when adding minus two—'

'What the devil are you talking about?'

'Señor, negatives can become confusing. If I say, "Is he not the man I did not see…?"'

'Can you appreciate the fact that one does not see a man one does not see?'

'But one can identify him by not seeing him.'

'If you are not drunk, Alvarez, you are providing a very good imitation of someone who is.'

The line was cut.

Alvarez replaced the receiver, slumped back in the chair and wondered if Salas was suffering from nervous exhaustion. Perhaps he would take early retirement. To be replaced by whom? Padilla or Gonzalez? Padilla was small-minded, intolerant, and overbearing, which must make him the favourite candidate...

The phone rang.

'The superior chief,' said the plum-voiced secretary, 'has asked me to say he wishes to know why you did not answer his call.'

'But ... but has he forgotten I've just spoken to him?'

There was a pause.

'He says it should have been very obvious he was referring to his previous call to your office.'

'There was no...' He remembered that the duty cabo had told him he was to phone the superior chief.

'Why did you not phone him as ordered?'

'I couldn't because I wasn't here until I arrived.'

'Repeat that.'

He did so.

There was another pause.

'The superior chief asks how could you be there before you arrived?'

'That's the point.'

'What is the point?'

'I couldn't.'

'He demands to know why you did not phone him the moment you did arrive.'

'I decided not to do so until I'd made a careful note of all I'd learned in order not to forget anything and because I did not yet have certain information, not having spoken to the persons concerned, being unable to do so.'

There was a long pause before Salas said: 'My secretary is showing signs of hysteria and refuses to speak further to you. So you will now report to me in the simplest terms of which you are capable, what you have been doing.'

'In order to decide whether Señor Rook's death was accident or murder, motive is clearly very important. Is there someone who had a motive for his death? If so, murder has to be considered. If there is not, accident becomes more likely. There is the important question of the missing rail and I am pursuing that very thoroughly, but this is a task which will take a long time to complete because an inability to be certain cannot be held to be probable proof through the lack of evidence—'

'If this is your idea of a report couched in simple terms, I trust there is never reason to ask for one couched in complicated ones.'

'I am trying to cover all aspects, señor.'

'Restrict yourself to those which are

251

relevant.'

'I have questioned several people. Señor Milne has a very attractive wife who has not remained faithful—'

'You will not pursue your perverse interest in matters which a normal mind avoids.'

'Her adultery is important.'

'To you, unfortunately.'

'She has been having an affair with Señor Rook and it seems that at the very least, Señor Milne suspected this which, of course, provides him with a motive; that is, if he is jealous of his wife's infidelity—'

'You suggest this could be doubted?'

'There are husbands who view their wives' affairs without rancour. Indeed, there are some who gain pleasure from watching—'

'Past experience has not prepared me for this. Your mind is an encyclopaedia of disgusting information.'

'It is a known fact, señor—'

'Known only to persons such as yourself. You will cease to crawl through the sewers.'

'Señora Milne was having an affair with Señor Rook; if Señor Milne discovered this, he had a very strong motive for murder.'

'Are you not contradicting yourself when you have just said that there are husbands ... I will not put it into words.'

'I said there were some husbands who did what you would prefer me not to mention again. I would not judge Señor Milne to be one of them.'

'In other words, you have raised the point merely to gain enjoyment from walking along paths others avoid.'

'In fact, it was you who raised it when you asked how I could doubt—'

'I intend to re-examine your file, Alvarez, to learn if there was a suggestion of mental abnormality when you were mistakenly accepted into the Cuerpo ... Do you believe Señor Milne murdered Señor Rook?'

'I don't think he did, but it's impossible at this stage to say he did not. It's always more difficult to prove the negative than the positive, isn't it?'

'You have always shown an ability to prove neither.'

'I have questioned Señor Carr.'

'Why?'

'He lost a considerable sum of money when he invested in a property development, initiated by Señor Rook, in Maracena. This loss has left him and his wife in financial difficulties. As far as I can understand, Señor Rook did not deliberately defraud Señor Carr, but Señora Carr is convinced he did and so, inevitably, he has begun to accept that.'

'I do not follow.'

'When a wife repeatedly claims something is thus, the husband slowly believes it is.'

'Only if he is of weak character and unable

to understand that women seldom have valid opinions on anything other than babies. If Carr is of so weak a character, it is most unlikely he would commit a murder which demands careful planning; his appreciation of the consequences of failure would very soon weaken the strength of his motive.'

'I agree with that.'

'I did not ask you for an opinion.'

'An additional reason for thinking him unlikely, however bitter, to have murdered Señor Rook is that he does not own a boat and there is no evidence of his having hired one ... I have also questioned Carlos Riera.'

'Who?'

'The fisherman who owns the llaüt—'

'The what?'

'It's a locally built fishing boat. Señor Rook's boat collided with Riera's and caused extensive damage which Riera cannot afford to have repaired. Riera was later heard to express himself in unambiguous terms—'

'Quote the exact words.'

'The owner of the boatyard to whom Riera was speaking suggested life works only for the rich and not the poor, to which Riera replied, "I'll teach the bastard" – meaning Señor Rook – "it doesn't." As I've mention-ed, his llaüt – his boat – is under repair, or it would be if he could afford that, but he surely would have no difficulty in borrowing a boat from one of his friends.'

'Have you questioned his known acquaintances to find out if he did borrow one?'

'Not yet, señor.'

'Have you asked him where he was at the probable time of Señor Rook's death?'

'He says he has little idea. And when I pressed him, he challenged me to say where I was and what I was doing at a certain time two months before.'

'And when you said you could remember perfectly?'

'I didn't.'

'Why not?'

'Because I could have no idea. Could you say where you were at fourteen hundred hours on the sixteenth of June?'

'My movements are not in question. An alert officer would never have made such an admission; he would have provided a positive answer in order to make Riera's refusal suggest guilt, thereby creating a psychological advantage.'

'Would that have been strictly ethical, señor? *The Manual of Field Practices* – which you ordered us to observe with meticulous care – is very firm that an officer in the Cuerpo must at all times speak the truth because the truth is his sword and shield.'

'Are you incapable of appreciating it is not intended that a member of the Cuerpo should view such imaginative language in practical terms? It is employed simply to bolster, when necessary, the Cuerpo's image in the public's eyes. Is there any indicative evidence of Riera's involvement in Señor Rook's death?'

'None has come to light. There is motive and opportunity, but as yet, no execution.'

'Which means you need to invest a great deal more effort into the investigation.'

'I am working all hours God made.'

'He did not make the hours, man did; illogically, of course, since we use the decimal system and therefore there should be twenty hours in a day, not twenty-four.'

'I think there are twenty-four because the Sumerians or was it the Babylonians—'

'An efficient officer does not waste his superior's, or his own, time on matters of no consequence. Kindly tell me what else, if anything, you have done.'

'I have begun the task, which unfortunately will almost certainly be a very long one, of finding where the length of rail was taken by Señor Rook to be repaired. This is very important. If it was never collected, then it was not used as a weapon and the blow he suffered could have been caused by falling on another section of the rails – leaving no traces sufficient to be observable – probably close to the missing section since there was this gap, making it far easier inadvertently to tumble into the sea.'

'You have not yet established where the rail

was taken?'

'The possible places where the repair could have been carried out are very numerous. Enquiries have to be made at each one, which takes time.'

'An efficient officer makes time his servant, not his master. You will take steps to conduct your enquiries far more efficiently and quickly. Is that quite clear?'

'But in the circumstances—'

'Have you anything more to report?'

'There is one person I must question again because of certain information. Until it can be determined whether it was accident or murder, I feel one should assume murder. In which case, Señora Rook must be considered a possible suspect. Now it is confirmed her husband is dead, she will benefit under the life insurance. That is, of course, if their attempt to carry out the fraud does not affect her claim. That will be a matter for the English courts. Would you know, señor, how they are likely to view the matter?'

'I have not the slightest idea. Civilized countries base their judicial systems on Roman law, the British, on something they call common law. That is a system in which error is multiplied almost as prolifically as ambiguity.'

'I have read that it provides a more flexible and therefore potentially equable system...'

'Good law demands certainty.'

257

'Before justice?'

'An absurd question.'

'It may be that whatever the doubts, the insurance company cannot prove a case in court because now that Señor Rook is dead, it is only circumstantial evidence which points to his fraudulent intention—'

'I should like to return home before midnight. Restrict yourself to relevant matters.'

'Señora Rook was in the ideal position to murder her husband and make it appear to be an accident; she knew he was going to set up the insurance fraud and how he was going to carry it out. So she forced him overboard, abandoned the boat and returned ashore in the small inflatable—'

'Where is the proof that she was aboard the boat?'

'There is no proof, as such, but there is the strong possibility when one remembers what Miguel Zapata said. Initially, I paid little attention to his words—'

'Why?'

'He is a man of very limited mental ability.'

'Yet you are prepared to give credence to his evidence?'

'A fool can sometimes foolishly speak wise words.'

'Unfortunately, in your case that gives me little cause for optimism. If you paid small attention to what he said at the time, why should you give it any heed now?'

'He spoke incoherently about a beautiful lady who gave him presents when she saw him, the package he had helped Señor Rook take aboard which had split open to reveal the small inflatable, the five euros he was given to forget what he'd seen. At the time, I accepted Señor Rook had given Miguel the money to persuade him not to mention the inflatable. But I have been asking myself, what if that is a false assumption? Suppose it was the "beautiful lady" who tried to buy his silence. Señora Rook is a beautiful woman. Perhaps Miguel saw her board the *Corrina* before Señor Rook arrived at the quay, so the señor had no idea his wife was aboard when he sailed.'

'The insurance fraud must fail if they were both aboard.'

'He had provided himself with the inflatable in which to go ashore, leaving the boat's tender aboard to make accident seem probable. She could have paddled ashore in the inflatable and then used whatever means of transport he had hidden to return to Son Raldo. In due course, she reported her husband had not arrived at Mahon.'

'Have you questioned the staff to find out if anyone saw her leave or arrive back that morning?'

'This is a line of enquiry I have only just begun.'

'You would explain slackness by incompetence? ... Why should Señora Rook kill her husband when they would have enjoyed the insurance money together?'

'I suspect she discovered he was shopping around.'

'What does shopping have to do with her motive?'

'Shopping in the sense that he was entertaining when she was away.'

'Alvarez, you are conducting an investigation, not carrying out a social survey.'

'Señor, he was entertaining other women.'

'I see. Like a vulture drawn to a carcass, you eagerly seek possible evidence of a certain nature.'

'Surely it is a detective's task to learn about the lives of those he is investigating, since their behaviour may provide the answers to questions?'

'It is beyond coincidence that the questions you concern yourself with are so frequently of a sexual nature.'

'When women and men are together, sex often occurs.'

'A claim which provides an unwelcome lens into your mind.'

There was a silence.

'Do you intend to leave your report unfinished?'

'In what way, señor?'

'You have not completed your interpretation of the señora's murder of her husband.'

'I think we should assume his death was accidental—'

'Are you incapable of logical thought? A moment ago, you were assuming his death to be murder.'

'Quite so, señor, but having made that assumption and that she killed him, one is led to the possibility it was an accident—'

'You are incapable of logical thought.'

'Señora Rook is a very attractive and desirable woman—'

'You will not pursue the matter.'

'Because of her physical advantages, her humiliation must have been all the greater when she was forced to accept her husband had been enjoying the favours of other women. A plain woman must expect her husband to stray—'

'Is the conception of marital faithfulness quite beyond your understanding? Are you unable to appreciate there are many who regard marriage as the covenant to which they swore allegiance at their marriage?'

'Husbands do stray.'

'So do skunks.'

'I don't think there are many skunks on this island—'

'Must you waste my time?'

'Señor, it is you who objected to my pointing out Señora's sense of humiliation would be all the greater because she is so attractive; attractive women expect to claim men's total

261

attention and their anger and concomitant humiliation is all the greater when they do not. When Señora Rook boarded *Corrina*, she thought, in the muddled way in which women's minds work, she would face her husband and threaten that if he ever again had an affair, she would expose the insurance fraud.'

'And inculpate herself?'

'She could claim she had not understood what her husband had been doing. In any case, she would not have been thinking clearly. *Corrina* sailed. At sea, she appeared suddenly, no doubt to the utter surprise and consternation of Señor Rook. Shock can induce anger. Perhaps he struck her, furious her stupidity might have endangered the fraud. She defended herself by lifting out the length of rail and struck him a blow on the head, following which he fell into the sea. There is an alternative, perhaps a more plausible one. He had removed the length of rail and had gone over the stern to fit the length of net about the propeller and was still in the water when she appeared. Overcoming his surprise, furious, he started to board. She saw a man who had betrayed her while she had accepted the risk of conniving with him in the perpetration of a fraud; a man who had lied every time he'd proffered his love for her; a man who was worth a million pounds dead. As he boarded, trying to subdue her rage with soft words, she struck him with the rail, knocking him back into the water. She sailed off, leaving him to drown.

'She abandoned *Corrina* and paddled ashore, used whatever transport he had hidden – probably a Mobylette since that could easily be hidden – to return to Son Raldo.'

'Proof?'

'As I have mentioned, until now I have not viewed the señora as a major suspect and so have not questioned her in depth.'

'Had you been more fully awake, you would have done.'

'It was when it seemed only Riera had both the motive and the means to murder, yet he presented an unlikely murderer where cunning was needed, that I remembered Miguel Zapata.'

'An efficient officer does not forget anything since he understands it can be the seemingly irrelevant detail which proves vitally important to the investigation. This case has already occupied too much time, so you will question Señora Rook immediately.'

Alvarez checked the time. Twelve fifteen. If he drove to Son Raldo, he might well be late home for lunch. 'I will go this evening, señor.'

'You did not hear me say "immediately"?'

'Just before you rang, I decided the señora

must be questioned, but when I phoned to make certain she would be at home, I was told she had left earlier and was not expected back until the early evening. I intend to question her then.'

'Why is it that whenever you are concerned, nothing can ever be done quickly?'

'That Señora Rook won't be home until later is hardly my fault.'

'It would not surprise me to learn that it was,' Salas snapped, before he cut the connexion.

Twenty-three

Alvarez rang the bell and waited. Marta, looking flustered, finally opened the front door. 'Is the señora here?' he asked.

'Went out to lunch and not returned.'

Fact imitating fiction, he thought, as she brushed back from her sweaty forehead a tangle of hair. 'And Señorita Rook?'

'Isn't here either.'

'Do you know where she is?'

'Couldn't say. I'll tell them you came.' She began to close the door.

'Hang on, I've some questions to ask you.'

'I've said all I can.'

'I'm sure you'll find something more to tell me.' He stepped inside.

'What do you want, then?' she asked sullenly. 'But be quick because I've work to do.'

The hall was air-conditioned, but his legs were tired. 'Let's find somewhere to sit and I'll explain.'

As she hesitated, a young man came through a doorway at the far end of the hall, stopped abruptly.

'Mario's my cousin from Andratx,' she muttered.

'A pleasure to meet you,' Alvarez said with formal courtesy.

Mario mumbled something.

'I presume Luisa and Diego aren't here?'

'What if they aren't?' she asked, with weak aggression.

'I'll have to come back another time to have a word with them.'

'What's going on?' Mario demanded.

'He's Cuerpo,' she answered.

Mario hurriedly returned the way he had come.

'He's my cousin from Andratx,' she said.

'So you mentioned. An attractive part of the island where the foreigners haven't ruined it. Now, shall we find somewhere to sit?'

She led the way into a small room that had the appearance of being seldom used and furnished with articles not wanted anywhere else. He sat in a chair which had seen hard service, but was remarkably comfortable. Once she was seated, he said: 'I want you to think back to June the sixteenth.'

'Why?'

'So you can tell me what you remember about that day. It was when the señor sailed from the port to go to Menorca. Where were you?'

'Here, I suppose.'

266

'You are not certain?'

'Of course not, after all this time.'

'It was a Wednesday.'

'Then I must have been here because I mostly only get half Saturday and Sunday off work.'

'Do you remember the señor leaving here?'

'No.'

'Or when the señora left the house?'

'No.'

'Perhaps you remember her returning?'

'When it's a lifetime ago?'

'I know, it's very difficult. Let's see if there's some way of jogging your memory. Is there a time around that date which would give you a base from which to work – perhaps a birthday. Did you or your cousin have reason to celebrate?'

'I didn't know him then...' Her expression of consternation was amusing. She hurriedly tried to escape her gaffe. 'Can you tell me what you were doing that day?'

'Yes.'

'I'll bet you're only just saying that.'

What would Salas reply to that jibe? 'I imagine you don't expect the señora or the señorita to return soon?'

She spoke uneasily. 'She ... she doesn't mind me meeting someone.'

'But would, perhaps, prefer you not to entertain your cousin in her house?'

'Please, you won't tell her, will you?'

'Not unless there's a reason to do so.'

'Nothing happened.'

'I'm sorry the earth remained steady.' He was also sorry she clearly failed to appreciate his gentle humour.

He left a few minutes later, knowing he was going to have to persuade Salas that this one line of enquiry would be fruitless since no one would remember anything of consequence about that Wednesday. Yet how else to uncover the truth?

Because of the cool of the house, the heat outside was magnified. A reflection of life, he thought sourly. Pleasure was always shadowed by pain.

As he entered the sitting/dining room, Dolores stepped through the bead curtain. 'You usually return before now,' she said, her tone sharp.

'I had to question someone at Son Raldo.'

'And, doubtless, had the answer been what you had hoped, you would not have bothered to return.'

'I was questioning one of the staff; no one else was there.'

'Which is why you have returned.'

Alvarez sat, leaned over to open the sideboard and bring out a bottle of brandy and a glass. 'Is there any ice?'

'In the refrigerator.'

In the old days, his enquiry would have

indicated he wanted some ice, so she would have hurried to fetch it for him; now, he was left to get it for himself even after a day's work. He stood and followed her into the kitchen which was not the place in which to voice his resentment. 'Something smells good,' he said. 'Is it pato a la Sevillana?' Duck, in expert hands, provided a Lucullan meal.

'Arros amb forn.'

Not a dish to decry – rice with pork and tomatoes – yet not one to make a man's mouth tingle with anticipation. He opened the refrigerator, brought out a tray of ice, emptied three cubes into his glass.

'No doubt you will hurry away as soon as you have eaten?' she said aggressively.

'As a matter of fact, I do have to question someone else.'

'Then you must hope she provides welcome answers.'

He returned to the other room, sat, poured himself a large brandy.

Marta opened the front door of Son Raldo. 'My God! Not you again!'

'One can never have too much of a good thing. Is the señora here?'

'Came back an hour ago.'

'I'll have a word with her then.'

'If you want. But she's been drinking, which always puts her in a foul mood.'

269

It was an unexpected bonus – drink loosened tongues. 'And is the señorita also back?'

'No.'

Gail had been away since the morning. With a friend? A male friend? A male friend, handsome, witty, of her own age, who knew the touch of 500-euro notes? He stepped into the hall, shut the door.

'You will remember, won't you?' she asked in a low voice.

'I've already forgotten what it is you're talking about.'

'In her present mood she'd ... I don't know what she'd do.'

He followed her into the large sitting room. Gloria was watching television on a large flat screen. By her side was an occasional table on which was an ice bucket, a bottle of champagne, and a half full flute. 'What the hell do you want now?' she demanded.

'To speak with you, señora,' he answered.

'I'm busy. You can come back some other time.'

'I'm afraid not.'

She picked up her glass and drank.

He had waited long enough to be invited to sit, so he sat. 'Would you turn off the television, please?'

'I'm watching.'

'I find it very difficult to talk when it's on and I'd prefer to speak with you here rather than at the post. You would be much less comfortable there.'

She refilled her glass, replaced the bottle in the ice bucket, switched off the television with the remote control.

'Thank you, señora. As you know, I have to determine whether or not the very unfortunate death of your husband was due to an accident.'

'You said it wasn't.'

'That there was the possibility it was not. Which is why I asked you if there was anyone who greatly disliked him.'

She drank. When she spoke, the occasional word was slurred. 'They all disliked him because he was so successful and because they reckoned he wasn't one of them. Made me bloody well laugh. Can't stop talking about the important lives they'd led and all the important people they'd known, while all the time they have to make certain they smile at their bank manager. And the women!' She drank heavily. 'Cucumber sandwiches and croquet in silly hats, that was their world back in England. But they're driving old SEATs and Opels and I'm driving a new BMW and there's also a Mercedes in the garage.' She drained the glass.

He was going to have to question her quickly and directly since she was approaching the fine line which separated the loose tongue from the lost one. 'I think you know

271

Señora Milne?'

'Everyone knows that tart.'

'You do not like her?'

'What's it to you?'

'Do you dislike her because of your husband's friendship with her?'

She emptied the bottle into her glass, only half filling it. 'Tell them I want more.'

He did not immediately move.

'Christ! You have to do everything for yourself these days.' She stood, held on to the back of the chair for support, walked erratically across to the wall and pressed the bell-push. Her return to the chair was an imperfect zig-zag.

'Señora Milne wasn't your husband's only affair, was she?'

She picked up her glass with a shaking hand and emptied it. 'He thought I didn't know. Bloody fool! A woman always knows.'

Was that true?

The door opened and Marta entered.

'Another bottle,' Gloria said.

'And for the inspector?'

'What's that?'

'What does the inspector wish to drink?'

It was not a chance to be missed. Alvarez said hurriedly: 'A coñac, please, with just ice.'

Marta left. Followed by his unspoken thanks.

'Señora, did it upset you very much when

272

your husband interested himself in a woman much less beautiful than yourself?'

His crude praise unlocked a corner of her mind. 'I asked him why he was chasing the bitch, what was she offering I didn't? I said, couldn't he see what she was after? He tried to tell me he wasn't screwing her. I laughed in his face.'

'You couldn't persuade him to end the affair?'

'He promised me he would. I knew he was lying.'

'You must have found the situation humiliating?'

'Of course I bloody did.'

Marta returned. She handed a very well filled balloon glass to Alvarez, lifted out of the ice bucket the empty bottle of Veuve Clicquot, wrapping a drying-up cloth around its base, replaced it with a full one. She turned to leave.

'For God's sake, woman, are you that stupid?' Gloria demanded angrily. 'Open the bottle.'

'Let me do that.' Alvarez stood and as Marta hesitated, crossed to the table, lifted out the bottle.

'Can't you see it's dripping everywhere?' Gloria said angrily.

Marta handed him the drying-up cloth. He would make a poor waiter. He stripped away the foil, unwound the wire cage, eased out the cork, remembered reading somewhere that in England one of the signs of proper breeding was that one never filled a champagne glass full and only half filled this one.

'Who told you to stop?' Gloria demanded. 'Anyone would think it was your champagne, not mine.'

He filled the glass. Here was confirmation neither of them was properly bred. He returned to his chair. It was a good cognac – the same marque he had had before. 'One becomes very angry when one is humiliated,' he said quietly. 'And your humiliation increased because you knew he was lying to you. So what did you do?'

'Told him I wouldn't continue if he didn't pack her in.'

'Continue with what?'

'Mind your own bloody business.'

Continue with the insurance scam. And Rook had given in to her demand. Except he hadn't and she'd discovered he was lying once again ... When she went aboard *Corrina* early that morning, had she been too emotionally confused to realize the stupidity of what she was doing or had she intended to make one last, desperate, impassioned appeal? Had her sudden appearance provoked a violent row? Or previously, had her mind already moved on to revenge and gain? 'Your husband sailed in the middle of the morning. Did you go down to the port before he left here, board the *Corrina*, and hide yourself?'

'What are you talking about?'

'Do you know Miguel Zapata?'

'No.' She emptied her glass.

'He works at the boatyard.'

She refilled her glass, spilling champagne on the table. At the second attempt, she replaced the bottle in the ice bucket. She drank.

'He says he knows you.'

'Then he's a liar.'

'Perhaps you do know him, but not by name. He's simple minded.'

'Like everyone else on this primitive island.'

'You gave him five euros and asked him not to say he'd seen you go aboard.'

'I don't know any halfwit and if I did, I wouldn't hand him five euros to spend on cheap booze.'

'Some time after *Corrina* sailed, you left your hiding place. Where was your husband when you first saw him?'

'You're talking crap.'

'For the insurance fraud to be successful, your husband had to be on his own. But you were too emotionally upset, too angry, too humiliated, to recognize that. Did he curse you for endangering or even ruining the projected fraud? Did he taunt you, say Señora

Milne was much more adventurous in bed than you? Did you lose your temper and attack him?'

'I wasn't on the boat!' she shouted. 'If I had been, I'd have saved him.'

'Ensuring your humiliation continued? You saw his death as providing revenge and the opportunity to enjoy what a million pounds could buy – the certainty that the next man you chose would have reason to remain faithful. You struck him with the length of rail, he fell into the water, and he drowned.'

'I wasn't on *Corrina*.'

'You are lying.'

'I swear I wasn't.'

'Swear on a stack of bibles and you'll still be lying.'

'Can't you understand? I was...'

'Well?'

'With someone else,' she muttered.

'Name the person.'

'I won't.'

'Because you can't. There is no such person. You were on your boat as your husband drowned.'

'I tell you, I'd have saved him. But I could not because ... because I was with...'

Her voice had dropped until he could not understand her last words.

'You were with whom?'

She emptied her glass, refilled it, drank. 'Errol,' she finally said.

'Is that a christian or a surname?'

'Errol Fleming.' She began to cry.

'Where does he live?'

'You mustn't see him.'

'He has to confirm what you have just told me.'

'But he ... he's married and she has all the money and if she ever learns that Errol and me...' Her voice rose. 'Maurice was with the Milne bitch, so why shouldn't I have some fun?'

'A question no one but you can answer. His address?'

As she finished telling him, her voice uneven, Gail hurried into the room. She stared at Gloria, then turned to face Alvarez. 'How could you?' she asked harshly. 'Are you sick? Do you get pleasure out of hurting people?'

'You don't understand—'

'You've been bullying Gloria because you don't give a damn about other people. You'd better leave.'

He left.

The villa spoke money. To build on a sloping site was considerably more expensive than on the level, the house was large and rock-faced, the front door was elaborately panelled in richly hued wood, in the garage was a Volvo estate and an MG sports car.

The door was opened by a tall, thin man with a sharply receding hairline, an apology of a moustache, and, as Alvarez silently named them, rat-like features.

'Señor Errol Fleming?'

'Yes?'

'My name is Inspector Alvarez of the Cuerpo General de Policia. I should like to speak to you.'

'At a time like this?' His tone was condescendingly aggressive.

'I am sorry, but the matter is important.'

'Nevertheless, perhaps you'll come back when it's more convenient for us.'

'Señor, do you know Señora Rook?'

Clearly shocked, he looked behind him at a closed door, then tried to bluster. 'Of course I do, same as I know the other English who are worth knowing.'

'Señor, if you cannot help me now, I shall have to question you at another time when perhaps the señora will be present.' He paused for several seconds, then said: 'Have you enjoyed an affair with Señora Rook?'

Fleming's expression was that of a man who had been hit in the solar plexus.

'Well?'

He finally managed a mumbled: 'Of course not.'

'Then Señora Rook is lying?'

'She ... she said that she and me ... Why would she say such a terrible thing?'

'Perhaps she did not find it so distasteful as you appear to do.'

278

'We ... we have been quite friendly.'

'That often is the case in such circumstances.'

'You don't...'

'What do I not do, señor?'

'You don't understand.'

'Then I will try to clear my mind by asking simple questions. Have you had sex with Señora Rook?'

'For God's sake, keep your voice down.'

'Unless you answer me, I will soon be tempted to start shouting.'

'We ... Maybe once or twice.'

'You cannot be certain?' It seemed the English failed to enjoy themselves even in adultery. 'Did you meet the señora on June the sixteenth?'

'How can I answer when that's some time ago?'

'It was the day on which Señor Rook sailed from the port to go to Mahon.'

'Oh!'

'You can now remember the day?'

A door opened and a woman, her face expressing autocratic superiority, looked out and said: 'Who is it?'

'A ... a policeman,' Fleming replied.

'What does he want?'

'I'm not certain.'

'Then tell him to go away. The programme's just starting.'

'Yes, dear.'

279

She shut the door behind her.

Fleming was sweating, despite the air-conditioning.

'Do you remember that day, señor?'

'My wife went into Palma to play bridge with friends.'

'Leaving you to play your cards?'

'What do you mean?'

'My apologies. Did you see Señora Rook that day?'

'We ... we went for a sail.'

'You have a boat?'

'Actually, it's my wife's.'

'When did you and Señora Rook meet and when did you part?'

'After Maurice had left, she rang and we met, drove over to Playa Neuva, which is where we keep the boat.'

'When did you return?'

'Gloria ... Mrs Rook ... said she had to be back home before Maurice arrived in Mahon because he was going to ring her to say he was safe.'

Alvarez thought for a moment, decided there were no more questions. 'Thank you, señor.'

'That's all?'

'For the moment.'

'I'd ... I'd rather you didn't come back.'

'If wishes came true, señor, we'd all be happy.' He began to cross to the door.

Fleming said plaintively: 'What am I going

to tell my wife is the reason for your coming here and asking so many questions?'

'As you must have successfully lied to her many times in the past, you will probably have no difficulty in doing so again.'

He returned to his car. The longer a man lived, the more inexplicable he found women. What could have persuaded some-one as attractive and desirable as Gloria to have an affair with that unprepossessing bean-pole of a man?

He drove off. He swore, employing his full repertoire of imaginative, obscene, scatological, and blasphemous Mallorquin expressions. Because he had deluded himself into believing he had solved the case, he had accused Gloria of murdering her husband, but Fleming's evidence made nonsense of that accusation and a witless fool of him for having believed he had discerned relevant truth in the jumble of words Miguel Zapata had spoken. Because he had been a witless fool, Gail would never wish to speak to him again.

Twenty-four

Saturday was usually a day of internal sunshine since work ceased as soon after midday as seemed safe; this Saturday was a day of black-bellied clouds.

'What is wrong?' Dolores asked.

Alvarez, seated at the kitchen table, tore off a piece of coca and dunked it in the hot chocolate. 'Nothing.'

'You are sitting there looking as if the world has ended for no reason.'

He ate. The coca tasted stale, the hot chocolate, bitter.

'Why are men such fools?'

He wished he knew the answer.

'Why cannot you accept you are no longer young?'

'I am not old.'

'You imagine a young foreign woman looks at you and sees someone young, slim, and handsome?'

'I don't give a damn what she sees.'

'I suppose she has found someone else and you are too blind to understand why.'

'If I am feeling low, it has nothing to do

with any woman. It's work that concerns me.'

'As my dear mother used to say, a man will plead poverty as he buys himself another drink at the bar. Aiyee! and how right she was when she also said, a man cannot find the woman inside.'

'Would we were given the chance more often,' he said sourly.

She rested her hands on her hips as she held her head high with Andaluce scornful pride. 'My cousin has the mind of a peasant from Mestara and so it cannot occur to him I was saying a man never appreciates the truth of a woman because he judges her only on appearance.'

He dunked another piece of coca.

'When you see a young, attractive, slim foreign woman, what do you do?'

'Nothing.'

'You run after her as quickly as your ageing legs permit. When you see a foreign woman who is not so young and is plain, what do you do?'

'Nothing.'

'Exactly. You ignore her because you are blind to her true beauty – honesty, kindness, loyalty.' She brought out a saucepan and a plancha from a cupboard and banged them together to underline her feelings.

'Will you ever understand I am not chasing a young, glamorous foreign nymphomaniac?'

he muttered.

'Did not Eloíse see you trying to hide in the club because you were with a painted woman half your age?'

'She is older than that, she wears very little make-up, and the only reason we were having a coffee together – as I've told you before – was because I had to question her. I have hardly seen her since then and won't be seeing her again.'

'She has found someone of her own age?'

'Why do you keep going on about age?'

'Because I am stupidly optimistic and hope that one day you will understand an old dog should have enough sense to lie down in the sun and not chase after young bitches ... Are you not going to work this morning?'

'It's Saturday.'

'Even so, you will soon be so late arriving at the post, it will be impossible to leave early.' She opened a store cupboard and searched amongst the contents. 'I thought I would make panada de carn i carxofes for lunch.'

'Good.'

'That is all you have to say?' She banged a tin down on the centre table.

He ate the last piece of coca. 'Is there any more?'

'A small portion in the cupboard. I suppose you expect me to get it for you?'

He did not deny that.

As she put the coca on the table, the phone rang. 'You expect me to answer?'

He did not deny that.

She hurried out of the room.

His thoughts became ever more bitter and self-censorious. He had had to question Gloria, but why had he done so so crudely? Why had he explicitly accused her of her husband's murder when really all he had had to rely on for that charge had been his own assessment of what Miguel Zapata had said? What could have promoted such hubris in him to believe he had divined important evidence?

Dolores returned. 'The call is for you,' she said, her words frosted.

He stood. 'Salas?'

'A woman who chose not to give me her name, but doubtless is the foreign woman whom you have hardly ever seen, will not be seeing again, and have not the slightest interest in what she thinks of you.'

He hurried through to the front room, picked up the phone.

'I'm having to make a habit of this, aren't I?' Gail said.

'It's the first time you've rung—'

'To apologize. I was horribly rude to you yesterday evening because I blamed you for the state Gloria was in. But later she calmed down and told me exactly what had happened. It was terrible for her when you suggested she had murdered Maurice, but I had eventually to understand you did so because your job demanded it. And so to accuse you of enjoying hurting people was monstrous; you'd never willingly hurt anyone. Can you ever forgive me?'

'I can't remember what you're talking about.'

'You really are a sweetie, Enrique. Will you let me try to make up for my behaviour? Can you meet me outside Club Nautico at eleven thirty?'

'Yes.'

'That's eleven thirty real, not Mallorquin, time.' She said goodbye, rang off.

The internal clouds had vanished and the internal sun was shining. He returned to the kitchen and sat; he ate the last piece of coca – as light as an angel's wing – drank the last of the chocolate – flavoured with nectar.

'Obviously, despite your protestations, you are seeing her again,' Dolores said sharply.

'Only to ask her some more questions.'

'The answers to which you hope you know.'

'Why do you think a man has only one idea in his head when he meets a woman?'

'Because there's no room for any other. When are you meeting her?'

'Soon.'

'Make certain you are not late back for lunch.'

286

He cleared his throat.

She stared at him, her dark brown eyes in challenging mode.

'I don't know what we're going to do,' he said.

'But you are optimistic?'

'It's just possible ... We may be having lunch together.'

'I see.'

'I'm very sorry.'

'Do not distress your imagination by trying to make apologies. I have become quite reconciled to the thoughtless behaviour of men who concern themselves solely with their own pleasures.'

He parked the car, stepped out, locked the doors, visually searched the quayside but failed to see Gail. He smiled. By telling him not to observe Mallorquin time, she had given him the chance to chide her for observing English time...

'Enrique.'

She was standing by the after rails of *Corrina*. She wore a loose-fitting shirt and shorts, again shorter than he would have wished because there were men who would eye her long, shapely legs with lascivious interest.

He crossed the quay. To board the *Corrina*, he had to climb the gangplank; reluctant to reveal his altophobia – that might be to diminish him in her eyes – he forced himself to display a courage that astonished him and mounted it with apparent confidence.

She met him as he stepped on to the deck. 'Gloria said I could take the boat out for a trip – of course, she'd no idea I was going to have you with me; that would have gone down like a lead balloon. I thought we'd sail around Cap Parelona and see a little of the north coast, so wonderfully dramatic it makes me wish I could paint. Then we'll return and anchor in one of the small coves and have the picnic Luisa has prepared. I've made certain there's plenty of brandy in the drinks' cupboard, so I hope all your desires will be met!'

His desires ... Dolores was right. He had a mind which ridiculously grew younger as his body grew older; he must become one old dog who lay in the sun and enjoyed memories, not hopes.

'Will you go back down on to the quay and stand by to cast off?'

Had she any idea of what she was asking? The fear he must again conceal...

'It's all right, there's no need for you to bother. Miguel will do it for us.'

She called to Zapata to ask him if he'd cast off. He nodded enthusiastically. 'Do you know Miguel?' she asked Alvarez.

'Very slightly.'

'What a tragedy! His life ruined when he

288

was young and now he has a miserable time with so many people treating him with contempt, unable to see he's a nice person; and then there's that awful man who runs the boatyard who won't pay him a proper wage even though I bet he's as good a worker as anyone else ... Damn!'

'Something is wrong?'

'I always give him a small present when I meet him, but I've only the two fifty notes I drew earlier. Have you five euros you can lend me?'

He brought several coins out of his pocket, picked out three coins and handed these to her.

She called Miguel aboard. He climbed the gangplank with confident speed, arousing Alvarez's sour admiration.

'Here's a thank you for helping us,' she said, as she handed Miguel the coins.

He stared at her with a reverence that was embarrassing to see.

'Go ashore now and cast off when I tell you.'

He pocketed the coins, descended the gangplank as nimbly as he had ascended.

'I'm going up to the flying bridge,' she said. 'Hoist the gangplank aboard and then stand by the after rope and haul it in when Miguel casts it off. And make sure it's clear of the screws. Go for'd and bring in the headrope.'

He watched her climb the short starboard ladder to the flying bridge, his thoughts now far bleaker than they had been earlier that morning. He would have raced up and down the gangplank a dozen times if to do so would have made certain Miguel had not appeared.

He hauled in the gangplank, a task his landlubberly awkwardness made difficult and physically demanding, yet for once he was grateful for the sweat of exertion. There were times when to suffer physically was a counter to mental suffering.

He made his way aft, his thoughts too chaotic and bitter to notice the slight vibration as the engines were started, or the watery burble of the twin exhausts. He had been both wrong and right. When Miguel had been talking about helping Rook with the package containing the small inflatable, the five euros *had* been given to him by a woman and it *had* been she, not Rook, who had asked Miguel not to mention her presence. But because Miguel had described her as beautiful and Gloria was beautiful and could be accorded a strong motive for Rook's death, she had become the prime suspect.

Alvarez stared down at the coughs of water from the starboard exhaust. He had failed to appreciate that Miguel, being simple, had the wisdom to recognize true beauty, whereas he, far from smart but not simple, had been attracted to Gail, yet had never thought of her as beautiful. As Dolores had said, he was blind to what was not obvious.

'Is the line clear aft?' Gail shouted.

The stern rope had been cast off and was trailing in the water. He hastily heaved it in and reported it clear. He went for'd and Miguel cast off the headrope; he hauled that in. Gail skilfully edged *Corrina* out from her berth, through the marina entrance, and into the bay. Soon, they were making sufficient way to create a light breeze which eased the heat.

'Are you going to stay there for the whole trip?' she called out.

He slowly made his way aft. He had responded to her virtues without recognizing them for what they were. Yet how could he now see in her loyalty, honesty, kindness? But she was the same person. Human relationships provided a maze simple to enter, almost impossible to exit...

He reached the starboard ladder, but did not immediately climb it. His incompetence encompassed more than an assessment of relationships. Why had he not remembered she had once mentioned her father's partnership and how he had lost all his money, but Rook had not? Should he not have wondered why initially she had, despite professed reluctance, provided information which identified the insurance fraud? (How he had tried to calm his own conscience because he was surreptitiously questioning her under the guise of friendliness! How she must have silently laughed at him as she passed on the information she wanted him to know!) Yet when Rook's death had been confirmed and it was possible he had been murdered, her only help had been to mention the missing rail which had been taken ashore to be mended. Why had he not accepted that if the lug of the rail had become bent – how? – then logically the rail would have been taken to the boatyard or to somewhere local so that once these possible sources of repair had been eliminated, it was necessary to doubt her story?

As he stepped on to the flying bridge, she turned. 'I began to wonder if you'd fallen overboard.' She smiled. 'Are you ready for a drink?'

'Yes,' he answered, his voice thick.

'Then I'll set up the auto pilot and we can go below.'

They had sailed around Cap Parelona and for a few miles along the north coast – a vista of stark, dramatic cliffs which falsely suggested an inhospitable island – then back and into Cala Roma, a curving cove, five hundred metres deep, whose steep, rocky sides were pine covered. Just before they dropped anchor, an Eleonara's falcon flew overhead and as the harsh noise of the chain interrupted the quiet, pigeons rose from the trees with clapping wings and a single golden oriole – a flash of yellow – crossed the cove. The water was crystal clear; fish, and briefly a small octopus, were visible. But the greatest attraction was the lack of any building or other human.

'Shall we swim before we eat?' she asked, as they stood in the saloon.

'I'm afraid I forgot to bring a costume,' he said. Deliberately forgot since he was well aware of the clumsy picture he presented in the water.

'Then we both go in skinny.'

It was as if an egg-beater had started up in his stomach.

'Embarrassed?' she asked provocatively.

'I ... I...'

'You ... you...' she mocked. 'Race you and the last one in is a prude.' She pulled her T-shirt up and over her head; she was not wearing a brassière. Her breasts were as provocatively shaped as he had envisaged. She undid three buttons on the side of her shorts, slid them down, stepped out of them. She was wearing cream-coloured, lace-edged pants. He found himself perversely wanting to look away in order to deny his salacious interest, yet remembering, with elated scorn, Dolores's assertion that he was

293

too old to attract a young foreign woman.

Naked, she walked aft and stepped over the stern on to the diving platform. 'How much longer are you going to dither?' she asked, before she dived into the water.

Twenty-five

They lay on the bed in the owner's cabin and the harsh sunlight came through one of the small ports to cross her body.

'When did you know?' she asked.

'Know what?'

'Don't be silly.' She moved her right arm and used finger and thumb to twist together some of the hairs on his chest. 'It was obvious you understood when I said I always gave Miguel five euros. Did you suspect before then?'

Why could they not have stayed in the bubble of time when there was beauty because there was no knowledge?

'Were you being rather slow?' Her tone was teasing.

'My superior chief would say I am a very slow person.'

'Only in some respects, my sweet Enrique. In others, you are a veritable cyclone.' She released his hair, raised herself up, leaned over and kissed him.

Twenty minutes later, lying on her back and staring up at the deckhead, she said: 'Do you understand why?'

'I'm not certain.' He watched the sunshine edge close to, then cover, the nipple of her right breast as the boat moved very slightly at anchor.

'My father led a very ordinary, ordered life; his brother, Maurice, one which could never bear close examination; we lived in suburbia, Maurice in smart areas with a succession of smart women. It was a complete surprise when he married Gloria because he was the archetypal sybaritic bachelor.

'A couple of years after the marriage, Maurice came to father and said he was in terrible financial trouble, he owed money to a man who had several painful ways of persuading a debtor to pay up. Father lent him all his available cash because although he disapproved of Maurice's lifestyle, he was his brother. Maurice didn't repay the money; instead, he returned and said he must have more, or Gloria's life was in danger. Father mortgaged his house, against my mother's strong advice, and gave Maurice what he'd asked for.

'Father died suddenly and mother shortly afterwards, from a broken heart – even if the medical profession won't accept that's possible. I asked Maurice for all the money he'd borrowed and he had the gall to say it hadn't been a loan, father had – against his advice – invested in a business in which he was interested. The business had gone bust and the money had been lost – he even added that his loss was greater than father's. I asked him how, if he was so hard up, he could live in an expensive house and Gloria continue to dress like a model. He was sorry I could think so ill of him as to believe he might be lying – and please would I never tell anyone else – but in truth they were living on the money Gloria had inherited.

'I couldn't prove the loan because there was nothing on paper. Despite all he knew or suspected about Maurice, father had believed there was absolute trust between them because they were brothers and that to ask for written confirmation of the loans would be to question that trust. I just had to accept that father had been swindled.

'I was left with very little capital – the house was worth little more than the mortgage because of a downturn in values – and since bad luck never travels on its own, the business for which I worked made half the administrative staff redundant in the name of cost-cutting and I was one of the unlucky ones. I had no home, no job, and very little money. Then Maurice turned up one day when I was feeling at the bottom of everything and said he'd heard I was in trouble – how he heard, I never discovered – and in the name of family ties, he wanted me to live with Gloria and him because then he'd know

I was not in want. He seemed so genuine I believed he meant it; that there was, after all, a warm as well as a rough side to his character and his conscience was more active than I would ever have thought possible. Gloria soon made it clear that conscience had played no part in the offer – she wanted a housekeeper. I wonder if you can have any idea of the snide subtlety with which she made me understand I was living off their charity?'

'I think I can,' he said, remembering how Gloria had spoken to her in front of him.

'Not long afterwards, they decided to move out here and I came with them. For a while, money was flowing, spent as much to impress as for their pleasure. But Maurice thought he saw a chance to make a fortune and invested heavily in a proposed development in Maracena; that suddenly went sour and he faced the loss of most of his capital and Gloria, the loss of kudos in an ex-pat society where background and breeding have taken second place to money.

'Living in the house, I gained hints of what was going on – overhearing telephone conversations, deciphering cryptic conversations – and realized Maurice intended to carry out an insurance fraud with Gloria's help.' She became silent.

He said slowly. 'So you...?'

'Hid aboard and when the boat was at sea

and he was about to abandon it, I appeared, giving him the shock of his life.'

'What was your intention?'

'Isn't that obvious?'

'You might have wanted to make him give up his attempted fraud. Or to make him pay the money he owed your father by threatening to expose him if he didn't.'

'What does it matter?'

'One action was honest, the other blackmail.'

She sat upright. 'I didn't expect you to turn hypocritical. You think I wasn't entitled to get back what was mine; that I should be prepared to sacrifice my own interests in the name of the law?'

After a while, he said: 'Did he lose his temper and attack you?'

She spoke calmly once more. 'I told him what I'd do if he refused to repay his debt by paying me some of the money he'd transferred to Liechtenstein. He laughed. Said he'd never expected a member of his brother's family to show such spirit; that I wasn't the conventional mouse he'd always thought me and he admired my camouflage; that I had far more to offer than he'd ever imagined possible.

'I didn't have time to wonder what he meant by that. He started pawing me. Can you begin to imagine what it's like to have your uncle fondling you; to have the hands of the man who swindled your father under your shorts; to have his moist lips pressing against yours, to have his tongue trying to force them apart? Of course I struggled. But he was so much stronger. I had to force him away, so I grabbed hold of the removable section of rail and hit him. He fell back and, because the rail was no longer there, into the sea. He was only semi-conscious, but making efforts to swim. I ... I went up to the flying bridge and sailed on. She was difficult to handle because he'd fixed the net around the propeller, but I didn't have far to go to where he'd chosen to abandon her. I went ashore in the inflatable, picked up the Mobylette he'd hidden amongst the scrub, and returned to Son Raldo.' She was silent for a moment, then continued, her tone harsh. 'I only wanted to fight him off me; it was all his fault; I'd every reason to leave him, but ... Oh, God! Enrique, I can't stop remembering his feeble, hopeless attempts to swim...' She pressed herself against him, seeking the oblivion of passion.

Alvarez braked to a halt in front of Son Raldo. Five minutes late. He smiled. Would Gail chide him for keeping Mallorquin time? He climbed out of the Ibiza, crossed to the massive front door, rang the bell.

Diego, looking as if he had had a heavy night, opened the door. 'More questions?' he asked sourly.

'Not this time. I've come to see Señorita Rook.'

'Then you're too late. She's gone.'

'Do you know when she'll be back?'

'No.'

Diego was venting his ill humour by being as unco-operative as possible. Rather than offer him the chance of any further perverted satisfaction, Alvarez decided to leave. Gail would get in touch and explain what had caused her to leave before he arrived. He walked back to his car, settled behind the wheel. As he started the engine, Marta came through the front door and across to the car, waving to catch his attention.

'The señorita told me to give you this,' she said.

He took the envelope. 'Do you know when she'll be back?'

'She took everything and she'd an airplane ticket, so maybe she won't be.'

As she returned into the house, he drove off, the letter on his lap. All the time the envelope was unopened, he could hope.

He finally drew over to the side of the road and switched on the hazard warning lights. He stared down at the envelope, hesitated, picked it up and opened it, brought out the single sheet of paper.

Her handwriting was neat, her words all too easily read. He would never betray her to the law, but she was certain he could never escape the knowledge that by remaining silent he betrayed himself. Because he was so honest, that knowledge would provide a mental burden he could never escape and inevitably it must sour their relationship. It had to be a thousand times better to have memories of a short, but sublime happiness, rather than endure a slow, growing resentment which could become hatred. So she was leaving the island. Gloria had had to give her some of the money she was owed and swear to give her the rest when the insurance money was paid, so she wouldn't starve. Never, never, would she forget their trip on *Corrina*.

He crumpled up the letter and threw it on to the floor of the car. Then leaned over, picked it up, smoothed it out, folded it and returned it into the envelope. He drove off.

Questions formed a whirlpool in his mind. Would Rook really have tried to have sex with her on the *Corrina* after having lived in the same house for years and never making a pass? Could her sudden appearance on the boat have inflamed desire as well as provoked shock? Or was the truth far grimmer? Had she suffered so much that she pursued her revenge beyond her declared intention to force him to repay his debt? Had her passion aboard *Corrina* been genuine? Or could Dolores be right? Could Gail have seduced him because she judged that then he would never find the determination to honour his duty and arrest her?

He stopped the warning lights and drove off. If he were a weeping man, he would weep. But he wasn't. So he would find a bar.

Salas rang on Monday. 'I have received no report from you.'

'I am preparing it now, señor,' Alvarez replied.

'Then you will give me a brief résumé.'

'I think we can assume Señor Rook's death to have been an accident since there is no hard evidence to the contrary. It's logical to assume the rail would have been mended locally, yet no local firm mended it, so it is probable that he had the intention to have it repaired, but never got around to doing so. I see the sequence of events to be like this. Having reached the point off shore where he had determined to abandon his boat, he stopped the engines, lifted out the rail at the back with some difficulty because of the bent lug, went into the sea to wrap the net about the propeller. When that was done, he boarded, picked up the rail and was about to replace it, tripped, hit his head on the rail beyond the gap, fell sideways and, with nothing to constrain him, into the sea, the rail still in his hand. Being at best only semi-conscious, he could not immediately regain the boat. He would have drifted at a different rate to the boat so soon there was no chance he ever could reach it.'

'You are satisfied none of the suspects had any part in his death?'

'There is no proof that any one of them did, so yes, I am.'

'Your full report is to be with me before Wednesday. And you will not include any unwanted references. Is that quite clear?'

'Señor?'

'You will not indulge yourself by unnecessarily introducing matters of a sexual nature.'

'Sex has played no part in my investigation,' he assured Salas.